MURDER
IN THE KOLLEL

MURDER
IN THE KOLLEL

A
Lincoln/Lachler
Mystery

Melvyn Westreich

Laurel
Publishing

Murder in the Kollel

Copyright © 2017 by Melvyn Westreich

First Printing: 2017

ISBN - 978-0-692-88357-0

Laurel Publishing
24751 Sussex Street
Oak Park, Michigan 48237

Website:
www.mwestreich.wixsite.com/melvynwestreich

ACKNOWLEDGEMENT

To Burt and Sharon Cohen for their encouragement. To Carol Perecman for helping in the research. To Rivy Gordon for believing I could do it. To Phyllis Shapiro and Malkie Goldberg for helping in the proofreading and terrific advice. To my loving wife, Ada, and my family for their support.

DEDICATION

To Ada, for putting up with me.

My life, my love.

PROLOGUE

THE MURDERER SURVEYED WHAT had been accomplished and was very proud.

Rabbi Avraham Klein swayed gently back and forth suspended by the noose around his neck. The rope went over the water pipe and was secured to the basement support post. It was in the perfect position.

Getting the rabbi's heavy bulk so high off the ground had been the murderer's biggest concern. But with a little ingenuity problems could be overcome.

The rabbi had barely stirred when the noose was first put around his neck and only really woke when the murderer slid the noose closed crushing his wind pipe and closing off the blood vessels to his brain. The rabbi had opened his eyes and recognized the murderer, but by then it was too late. The murderer had apologized to the rabbi, "I'm sorry. It could not be helped. You left me no other option." But the murderer was not sure if the rabbi actually heard because he was thrashing about, grasping and pulling at the noose that was strangling him. All that ceased after a few moments.

The murderer placed the highlighter and the Bible on the table and looked around to see if everything was in its proper place.

A little more housekeeping was needed and then the murderer would be completely satisfied.

People would say, 'What a shame'.

'Rabbi Avraham Klein had committed suicide'.

CHAPTER ONE — Not What It Looks Like

THIS CANNOT BE GOOD.

Ephi was on a mission.

Ephi — short for Ephraim Salzberg — was the official bearer of bad news. He was not a student and not a rabbi. The forty seven year old bachelor had occupied the corner table of the *bais medrash* — *yeshiva* study hall — for decades. Not being a great Talmudic scholar ... far from it ... the rabbis of the *yeshiva* would call upon him to do various housekeeping chores; take attendance, chastise frivolous students ... stuff like that ... and deliver bad news. He was now weaving purposefully through the maze of tables of the *bais medrash*.

Someone was in trouble.

The learning dynamic of the large room was totally different from any study hall in any major institution of higher education. Study halls at the university were expected to be enveloped in an almost tomblike silence so that each individual could concentrate on the subject at hand.

The *bais medrash* was the exact opposite.

At each one of the sixty or so tables scattered around the large room there were at least two, and sometimes as many as six, *bocherim* — plural of *bocher* or student — who were chanting phrases out loud or making vociferous comments about the subject they were studying. Some were engaged in even louder arguments over the meaning of the phrases cited in the books they delved. My study partner, Shragai Halperin, was diligently, and yes, loudly, trying to teach me the logic of the Talmudic text we were studying. A glimmer of understanding seemed to be just beyond my grasp but was getting closer.

It suddenly dawned on me that Ephi could be heading my way.

I had a sudden sphincter spasm.

Sure enough, when he reached my table he ... Ephi Salzberg ... my personal *malach h'mavess* — Angel of Death — said officiously, "Lincoln, Rabbi Kalmonowitz wants to see you in his study." Then to emphasize the fact that he considered me to be in deep trouble, he added a command, "Now!"

The hub-bub at the tables around me died down and changed to an ominous silence.

Bad news.

Ephi turned and began walking back to his table, signaling with his hands to the silent students at the adjacent tables that they should return to their learning.

I could not be angry with Ephi. He was only the bearer of the bad news. It was not his fault.

It was mine.

I had been expecting this summons for the past eight months.

I guess I really was in deep doo-doo.

See how I have changed. Even when I think to myself, I say doo-doo instead of the s - word. Eight months ago the s - word and the f - word would have punctuated just about every other sentence. That was just one of the things that Rabbi Kalmonowitz said I had to work on if I was going to be a *chozer b'tshuva* — one who repents and returns to the ways of the Torah — and have any success in the *yeshiva*. He said that even in my thoughts I had to train myself to refrain from using words and phrases that were considered crass or crude. So I guess I really have changed.

Fat lot of good it was going to do me now. Rabbi Kalmonowitz was about to drop the hammer. And I was going to be the one that was blown away.

I think Shragai knows what the summons means and he just keeps looking at me in silence.

I closed my volume of the Talmud and gave it a respectful kiss as I put it on the pile at the corner of my table. I stretched and then arched my back which was stiff from sitting these last few hours. I grabbed my jacket from the back of the chair and put it on as I stood to my full six feet. I was not the tallest man in the *bais medrash* but at thirty seven, I was definitely the oldest of the *bocherim*. I was even older than some of the younger rabbis.

I closed the top button of my shirt and did up my tie. I pushed my *yarmulke* — skull cap — to the back of my head and covered it with my black fedora that had been lying on the table.

How appropriate.

For now, I was still wearing the official uniform worn by all the other *bocherim* in the *bais medrash* — white shirt, black hat, black suit, black shoes and black tie. It is a sight to behold. In order to imagine what we looked like, think Dan Aykroyd and John Belushi, dressed as Elwood and Jake Blues. Now multiply that by three hundred *bocherim*. Get rid of the iconic sunglasses and substitute in their place the fringes of the *tzitzis* — small prayer shawls — poking out from the *bocherim*'s pants.

You get the picture?

I thought to myself that a black outfit was just perfect for facing a firing squad.

Really appropriate.

This was only my second visit to Rabbi Kalmonowitz's windowless study at the center of the building.

I knocked and entered.

Nothing had changed.

The groaning shelves which covered the walls and every flat surface, held sets of books bound in leather or the classic blue or burgundy. All the remaining nooks and crannies were crammed full with single volume works. The gilded markings on the spines had been worn off long ago and the rabbi probably knew what each book was by its location in the room.

Rabbi Kalmonowitz sat behind his small desk intently studying a large copy of the Rambam — Maimonides. I had noticed that when the rabbi studied a text he had a nervous habit of slowly stroking his voluminous grey beard and every thirty seconds or so, he would adjust the black skull cap on his head. I could almost feel the wheels of logic that were shifting in his mind. His total belief in God coupled with his photographic memory and absolute mastery of Talmudic knowledge, filled me with a feeling of awe. Every time I looked at the rabbi I felt that I should be seeing some sort of visible aura or halo.

So far no halo but the awe still remained.

At first I thought that he was not aware that I had come in but he looked up momentarily from his text and said, "Please take a chair." He was sitting in his shirt sleeves, his frock coat and hat hanging from a peg jutting out from one of the shelves.

I wonder whether this is some sort of test that the rabbi sets to each of the guests that visited his room. Obviously he expected me to take the one chair positioned opposite his desk. The problem was that it was piled high with books. I suppose he wants to see whether I will just stand or try to find some place in the crowded room to accommodate the books from the chair. Last time I was here I decided to move the books and caused a minor avalanche. Once more I shifted the books and placed them on top of a gravity-defying stack already on the desk and hoped for the best.

God willing, it will not come tumbling down.

Once I was seated, Rabbi Kalmonowitz looked up and closed his book. He seemed to be forming the words in his mind before he spoke.

Here it comes.

"*Reb* Shimon," began the rabbi. He always called me by my Hebrew name with the honorific title of *Reb* ... a title I did not deserve. "I think you might know why I have called you here."

Of course I knew. Rabbi Kalmonowitz was going to throw me out of the *yeshiva* for being the dumbest *bocher* in the *bais medrash*. He had warned me from the start that he was not sure that I had the stuff needed to study in the *yeshiva*. He also told me that once he made up his mind, he would tell me straight out if I could or could not continue in the *yeshiva*. I knew from the outset that it was a really stupid move to try and start cramming my brain with material that should have been learned twenty years before. Even the slowest high school kid in the *bais medrash* knew more than I did. "Yes, *Rebbi* , I know," I said, staring down meekly at my shoes. I did not have the nerve to look into Rabbi Kalmonowitz's steely blue eyes.

"I thought you would," said the rabbi. "I am very pained by this whole incident."

Oh terrific.

I have caused him pain. Now I have got that on my conscious as well. He told me when I first came to him that not everyone needs to learn in a *yeshiva*. But I insisted. Now look at where we are. "I'm sorry, *Rebbi* . When do you want me to leave?" I guess the sooner the better.

"My, my, you are the clever one. As it says, who is a clever man, someone who can deduce an item from another item," said the rabbi with a chortle. "I don't know exactly, I will speak with Rabbi Lipsky and see what he has to say. Maybe next week. You'll need a place to stay in Lansing."

Who was Rabbi Lipsky? There was no one in the *Yeshiva* by that name. And where was I suddenly so clever? And what did he mean maybe next week? And what about

Lansing? "Excuse me, *Rebbi*," I interjected. "What does Lansing have to do with my leaving the *yeshiva*?"

A smile of understanding broke out on Rabbi Kalmonowitz's face, "Oh I see. You think I called you in to ask you to leave the *yeshiva*."

"Of course I did. I know my progress is extremely slow. You warned me that I might not be able to keep up. Isn't that what this is all about?"

"Shimon, Shimon, Shimon," said the rabbi in a soothing tone. "Of course your progress is slow. You are trying to make up ten years of missed learning in one. To you it seems slow. To me and your teachers your progress is amazing. When you first came you could hardly understand a word in Hebrew much less in Aramaic. Here it is eight months later and you are studying *gemarah*. It's phenomenal."

"So, you are not throwing me out of the *yeshiva*?"

"Absolutely not," said the rabbi with finality.

"Then what are we talking about?" I asked, totally confused.

"Let me try to explain," said Rabbi Kalmonowitz. "Did you hear about the death of Rabbi Klein from the *kollel* in Lansing?"

One of the *bocherim* had explained to me that a *kollel* was a free standing *bais medrash*, that usually did not have a direct affiliation with a large *yeshiva*. Small groups of Jewish scholars sat in them and learned all day. Some *kollels* had teaching programs for the community and some did not.

"I think I heard something about it a few weeks ago. Sorry, I am in the *bais medrash* most of the day and don't get to see the TV or newspaper," I apologized.

"To make a long story short, Rabbi Klein died last month and the police are convinced it is a case of suicide. I spoke with the police and they were very reluctant to give out any information but they assured me that they have concrete evidence."

I was getting an inkling as to why the rabbi wanted to talk with me. Before donning the Blues Brothers' outfit I had been a police detective and private investigator. I knew that it was a statistical fact that rabbis seldom committed suicide, but I also knew that the Lansing Police force was a highly professional group and if they were convinced that it was a suicide, it probably was. "How can I be of help?" I asked tentatively.

"Rabbi Klein was my *talmid* — student — and I knew him for over twenty years. He did not commit suicide," said the rabbi emphatically. "I don't know what happened there, but Avraham Klein did not take his own life."

"I see," I said slowly. "The police in Lansing are very good. It's hard to imagine they would make such a mistake."

"Nevertheless, they are mistaken if they think the death of Avraham Klein is a suicide," said the rabbi determinedly.

I cocked my head to one side and asked, "Where do I fit in with this whole thing?"

"As I said, this whole incident pains me," said the rabbi and then paused. "That Avraham Klein is no longer with us pains me greatly, but it pains me even more to think that perhaps there is someone that took *Reb* Avraham's life and is walking free. The holy books say '*Tzedek tzedek tirdofe* — strive for justice justice'. I want justice for my *talmid Reb* Avraham."

"The police might be right and it is a suicide. It could be."

"Then I will apologize to you and anyone else and accept my loss. What I am asking you to do ... and it is purely a request ... please turn me down if it makes you in any way uncomfortable ... I know it is a terrible thing I am suggesting. You are so dedicated to your studies. But I would greatly appreciate it if you would take a short recess from the *Yeshiva* and look into *Reb* Avraham's death. This is something in which you are an expert and I am the *am h'aretz* — boor. The *yeshiva* will cover your expenses. Whatever you discover I will accept. But until you tell me otherwise, I am sure ... absolutely sure ... Avraham Klein did not take his own life."

Rabbi Kalmonowitz stated quite clearly that he was only making a request and he said that I could turn him down, but a polite request from him was just like a command from anyone else. Sort of like the 'offer you can't refuse' from Don Corleone, but without the 'sleeping with the fishes' part. Most of all ... it was Rabbi Kalmonowitz making the request and I knew I could not turn him down.

Besides, after eight months of being the absolute dunce among all the *bocherim* in the *bais medrash*, it would help to bolster my ego — which was now resided in a bottomless pit — to show off a little by doing something I was good at.

If I had to say so myself, and I had commendations to back me up, I was a darn good detective.

Probably it would take only a day or two to sort through the material in the Lansing Police file and it would be a good break from the seven-day week, 24/7, intense study of the past eight months.

But most important ... absolutely the most ... I was not being thrown out of the *yeshiva*.

Whoopee!

"*Rebbi* , I would be more than happy to take a look at the case."

CHAPTER TWO — *Jumpin' Jack*

IT WAS MONDAY MORNING and it felt good to be behind the wheel of my GMC Terrain driving down I-96 on my way to East Lansing. I bought the car just two months before I entered the *yeshiva* and it had yet to hit 2,000 miles. For the past eight months I commuted to and from the *yeshiva* on my bike and only used the car to go shopping on the week-ends or to get through heavy snowfalls. Mostly the car stayed parked in the car port in front of my Southfield condo. I had forgotten just how much I enjoyed driving down the open highway.

Strange how you can adapt to just about anything.

The state troopers were out in droves and I set the cruise control to keep me just under the limit. Very likely, if I received any speeding tickets, my contacts through the 'old-boys' network could quash them, but why use up the credit.

When I took this 'case' I had to decide if I was going to continue wearing my *yeshiva* b*ocher* 'Black Suit' outfit during the investigation, or go under the radar with jeans and a T-shirt. I elected to go with the Blues Brothers' uniform.

When I started to learn in the *yeshiva* in earnest, Rabbi Kalmonowitz told me that I could come to the *bais medrash* in my regular clothes (i.e. sans black suit). But I figured, in for a penny in for a pound. The black suit was the uniform of the *yeshiva* team. If I wanted to be part of the team I had to get uniformed up.

With the exception of the *yarmulke* and the *tzitzis*, the black outfit has no inherent holiness. A Jewish man is expected to keep his head covered at all times and wearing the *tzitzis* is a commandment from the bible.

I feel that when I wear the uniform, people who see me immediately know who I am and what I am. It does the same for me. It helps define what is expected of me and how to behave and react.

 For some reason I thought the *yeshiva bocher* team uniform would be more appropriate to investigate the rabbi's death. He had been a part of the team.

I stopped at a highway rest area just after Brighton and when I went to the toilet I put on my jacket and black hat. When I came out about a half dozen people stopped and stared. They looked like they were trying to figure out if aliens were invading the planet. Few Michiganders ever see a *yeshiva bocher*.

I planned my trip so that my first stop was to check in to my hotel. Normally, when I was on a case, I would not worry about lodgings, but things had changed.

I now kept kosher.

No more burgers at McDonalds. No more KFC.

I do not do well on an empty stomach and anyone that keeps kosher and is 'blessed' with a big appetite has to plan their meals carefully. Kosher food does not grow on trees and Lansing was not known for its kosher food resources. I figured it would be a day or two or three before I could get back to Dave's Kosher Burgers in Oak

Park. So, before setting out this morning, I stopped at the One-Stop Kosher Market and loaded up with prepared meals, cold cuts and assorted nosherie. I also made an online reservation at the University Place Marriott, which was close to the police station and had special requested a microwave and fridge.

I checked in to the hotel and put my perishables in the fridge.

Since I had not had much of a breakfast and I had no idea how long I would be at my second stop — the East Lansing Police Department — I decided not to take any chances. Before I left my room I sliced open a bagel, slathered it with mustard and stuffed it full with sliced corned beef.

I get hungry ... I get antsy.

I hopped into my car and as I drove to the police station I wolfed down my bagel ... trying as best as I could not to get mustard on my white shirt.

Before leaving Detroit, I had called my former boss, Lt. Mike Gleason, at the detectives division of the Detroit Police Department and he said he would put in a good word for me with the detectives in East Lansing. If the police would cooperate, ninety percent of my work was done.

The station was housed in a modern two story building in a residential neighborhood just adjacent to the courthouse. Michigan State University, the big deal of the city, was a few blocks away. The detectives division was on the second floor and I asked a clerk to point me towards Lt. Al Walker, the name Lt. Gleason had given me.

The division was at the back of the building and no sooner had I entered their squad room when I heard a voice, that sounded like a board being dragged over gravel, say, "Slinky!!! Is that you?"

It was over seventeen years, but I recognized the voice immediately. Heck, I would recognize that voice until the day I died. There was only one voice like that.

John (Jumpin' Jack) Slatterly.

He was a classmate of mine from the Detroit Police Academy. He got his nick name from the calisthenics class because his coordination was so bad he could not do a jumping jack to save his life. He was also the one that coined my moniker, "Slinky".

Simon Lincoln ... S. Lincoln ... S. Linc ... Slinc ... Slinky. Get it.

I hated the name, but it stuck with me throughout the Academy. Once I graduated I insisted that everyone call me Sy. My first assignment was to the Palmer Park Station and I rarely saw Slatterly, but when we ran into each other he always called me 'Slinky'. When he left the Detroit Police, I sort of lost track of him.

I assumed that the name was dead and buried and that after seventeen years not a vestige or memory of it remained. But I forgot about Jumpin' Jack. I should have realized he had to be out there somewhere.

I turned towards the voice to see that John Slatterly was as big as ever. Actually, even bigger than ever. At the Academy, Jumpin' Jack had been big — height and width. The height was still the same, about six foot three, but the circumference had just about doubled and he was balding rapidly. I guess the physical requirements needed to stay on the force in East Lansing were a bit lenient.

John waddled over to me and gave me a big 'man hug' and a slap on the back. No smoochie smoochie girlie type hugs.

"Al gave me the heads up that you were coming out here to the boonies," said John. He stood back and took in my black suit and black hat and asked, "What? Are you becoming Amish or something? I almost didn't recognize you."

"No, I'm taking a break and studying in a Jewish *yeshiva* for a while," I replied.

"I heard about you getting shot and how you quit the force," said John sympathetically. "Now you're pulling in the big bucks in the private sector, down in Detroit."

"Thank God, I'm doing OK. I'm taking a break from work right now." Jumpin' Jack nodded in agreement. "Trying to find myself," I added.

"Find yourself? Crap, everyone could always find you. You were the biggest mother in the Academy," commented Slatterly.

"You mean, because I was the only one that could whoop your beeee-hind?" I said in jest.

Jumpin' Jack turned to face the half dozen people in the detectives division and said loudly, "Folks, meet Slinky."

Oh great, now that name has been resurrected.

"Former Detective Sergeant Simon Lincoln of the Detroit PD. Now a PI," continued Slatterly. "We went to the Academy together and he was the only one that beat me in hand to hand. He had been some sort of hand to hand expert in the Marines, so, he beat me. I mean really beat me. He is one bad-ass individual and I am happy to say he is my friend, because I would not want him to be my enemy. He's here looking at one of our cases and we are going to give him maximum cooperation."

Everyone said hello as they nodded, waved, or shook my hand before they went back to whatever it was that occupied their time. I just kept repeating to anyone that would listen, "Call me Sy ... call me Sy."

When it was just me and Jumpin' Jack again I asked, "People listen to you around here?"

"Yeah, this force has less than sixty officers and when I came up here from Detroit they thought I was a big deal. Now I'm a detective sergeant like you were and second in command in the division," said Jumpin' Jack, making a simple statement of fact. No bravado or ego.

That's just the way it was.

"Terrific. That's really great," I said earnestly. "Gleason called ... I was supposed to see Lt. Walker."

"Yeah, I know. Al told me. How is Mike?" asked Slatterly.

"He's fine. Going to retire next year, or so his wife thinks," I answered.

"He's a good guy." Pleasantries over, Slatterly shifted gears. "I hear you want to look at the Klein suicide."

"That's what I was asked to do," I said.

"Can I ask you why? It was as open and shut as they come. The guy said goodbye and went away. No foul play. Not even a whiff of it. So why the interest?" asked Slatterly.

"The people who hired me knew Klein very well and they feel that there is no way that he could have committed suicide. He's not the type."

"They're all the type. Things get tough ... something snaps ... and they become the type. You must have seen it dozens of times down in Detroit."

I nodded my head in agreement and said, "Sure I have, and you are probably right. And that is what I told the folks that hired me. So, let me look at the case file. It'll take me a day or two to check a few facts. I'll write my report and I'll be out of your hair ... or what's left of it ... in no time."

Slatterly stopped speaking for a moment and squinted his eyes at me, "Slinky? I know you are in the private sector now, but have you got any information that would change our decision on this suicide. You know I have to warn you that withholding evidence is a crime," he said earnestly.

"Jumpin' Jack, the only proven fact that I know about this case is that Avraham Klein is dead," I answered. "I know you folks are convinced that it was suicide and I respect your expertise in this. I will look at your file and if I learn different, you will be the first to know."

"OK, just wanted to get the ground rules straight," said Slatterly. "We will be glad to cooperate. You are going to get cooperation up the whazoo. Let's go to Lt. Walker's office ... he's out of town until next week and it will give us some privacy. And call me John or Slatterly."

Did I just see Slatterly wince when I used the name 'Jumpin' Jack'? Maybe he would like to make a trade. No 'Slinky' ... no 'Jumpin' Jack'.

CHAPTER THREE - Righteous Like the Pope

JUMPIN' JACK CLOSED THE door to the office and sat in his boss's chair. He pulled a seat up next to him so that we could both see the papers in the file. The cardboard folder was not very thick and he said, "This is a complete copy of the entire file. We left nothing out. That includes a disk with all the pictures at the scene and the video walk through of the house. You are free to take the file with you, just destroy it once you are through with it."

Standard police procedure ... when they were being cooperative.

"Thanks," I said.

He began speaking without needing to open the file before him, "Let's see. Quick rundown. Avraham Klein. Occupation — Rabbi. White male, forty five years old, no children, good health, no criminal record. Not even a parking ticket. Thirty four days ago, sometime before 10:45 pm, while he was dressed in his pajamas, he threw a noose over a water pipe in his basement and tied it off. He got up on a stool, put the noose around his neck and stepped off the stool. The Medical Examiner determined the time of death to be approximately 10:45 pm, give or take fifteen minutes. The body showed no signs of trauma other than the strangle marks made by the rope and some bruising of the heels of his feet — apparently from kicking around as he died. Perhaps from the stool.

At about 12:20 am, the wife discovered the body when she came home from watching a film at the cinema complex. She says she had no idea that he was contemplating suicide. The house is equipped with an old but competent security system and it was working fine on the night he died. The security company shows that no one entered the house from the time his wife left for the film until she returned. First responders arrived at the scene at 12:32 am, and secured the area. They found no evidence of forced entry or any signs of a struggle. In fact the entire house was neat as a pin. The beds were even made. There was no sign of poisons or noxious substances. All the security triggers on the doors and windows were intact and operational. A search of the rabbi's study showed a file with a number of brochures from private psychiatric institutions. When we checked those out we found that the rabbi had been in contact with them about an elective hospitalization. The wife corroborated this. And, oh yeah, the week before he died he notified his immediate boss … some rabbi … named Liper or Lansky … or …"

"Rabbi Lipsky," I said.

"Yeah that's the name. It's in the file. That he would have to take off some time to deal with personal issues. Like half a year."

"Half a year?" I asked.

"Yup. We also found a Holy Bible with a passage in Lamentations highlighted. Chapter 1, Verse 20. It was written in Hebrew and the translation is: 'See, O Lord, how distressed I am! I am in torment within, and in my heart I am disturbed, for I have been most rebellious. Outside the sword bereaves; inside is only death'. To us it looks like he was telling everybody he was going away." Slatterly turned to me and asked, "So tell me mister hotshot high salaried PI, what does this sound like to you? Murder one? Manslaughter?"

"Sounds like an open and shut case of suicide."

"Thank you. I rest my case."

"Did you do an autopsy?"

"Yes and No." Slatterly explained, "Medical Examiner made the call. Didn't think the case warranted a full autopsy and the wife nearly had a conniption fit when we suggested it. Only about twenty percent of our suicides get full autopsies. What they did was a closed autopsy. They ran the corpse through an ultrasound and CT machine and checked the body for drugs, alcohol, and poisons. It showed that all the internal organs were intact and confirmed the impression that there was no trauma other than what he had on his neck and the heels, which I mentioned before. You know, they can even put little TV cameras into just about any part of the body, but it wasn't needed in this case. These closed autopsies save the county a shitload of money."

"No enemies, bad debts, disputes?" I asked.

"Nope. Man was loved by all. As far as we can tell he was a flippin' saint. The community simply loved both him and his wife. Everyone said they were the most devoted couple around," said the detective.

I thought to myself that if this was not actually a suicide, then statistics said it was a ninety percent bet that the perpetrator was someone close to the deceased. So I had to ask, "Did you corroborate the wife's whereabouts?"

"Sure did. We checked her out completely. Name is Devorah, maiden name Gorelick, forty three years old, married Avraham Klein when she was twenty three years old. No children. No criminal record. No medical or psychiatric history. Her family is loaded and so is she. The house is in her name and all the family money. She basically pays all the bills out of her own stash. The rabbi had no insurance policies, so she had nothing to gain financially with her husband's death. She is considered to be a pillar of the Jewish community. People at the theater remember that she comes to see a film every Wednesday evening and they saw her there that night. Security tapes back that up. We got her cell phone server to check their records and do a GPS tracking for her phone that night. It shows she went directly to the theater when she said she did. She stayed in the theater the entire time and then returned directly home after the show." He said this last as a sort of challenge. Waiting for me to think of some aspect of the case that they had not investigated.

"What about a CSI report?"

"It's in the file. They found nada. Only prints in the house are from the husband or the wife."

"So far, it sounds like a suicide to me," I conceded.

"What did I say … are we righteous or what?"

"Righteous … Righteous … like the Pope."

"I know you are still gonna want to look at the file yourself, because that is what I would do. So here it is. Knock yourself out." He pushed the file towards me as he headed for the door.

I opened the file and asked, "Did you check his computer and phone?"

With one hand on the door handle he said, "Sure did. He had an old fashioned clam-shape phone so there was not much to get from that. We still have his laptop and home computer and the cyber guys went over them. Didn't find a thing."

"Would you mind if I had my computer guy check the hard disks?" I asked.

"We signed off on both disks and we were about to put them back into the computers and return them to the wife, so it would not break the chain of evidence for you to look at them as well. I'll tell her there is a slight delay. Three days OK? Just don't lose them."

"That would be great."

As he was leaving he said, "Slinky, didn't I tell you that you would get cooperation up the whazoo?"

"You sure did 'Jumpin' Jack'."

That stopped him at the door. He turned to me and said, "I get it ... Sy."

"I knew you would ... John."

"By the way, Julie Dalton was the lead investigator on this call." He turned to the squad room and spoke loudly to a forty year old black woman, "Hey, Julie."   The black woman looked up and he continued, "If my man here Slink ... I mean Sy ... has any questions you help him out." Julie nodded in the affirmative and Slatterly turned back to me, "I'll get you those hard disks now."

Slatterly left and I made a mental note that I had to speak with Rabbi Lipsky and *Rebbitzen* Klein. I had to read the file carefully and look at the pictures. I would need to see the basement where the rabbi died. But that all could wait. First things first. I realized that three days with the disks was not much time and I had to get them to my man in Detroit ASAP. I put in a call to Chuckie Short, the head of the cyber crimes division at the Detroit PD. He did some private work on the side and I had never found anyone who was better at unraveling the secrets of the computer.

My connection went through on the fourth ring and I heard the very loud, "Yo! Speak to me." This was Chuckie's standard way of answering his phone. It didn't matter if you were the janitor or the Chief of Police.

"Chuckie, it's me Sy."

"Sy Lincoln. Under what rock have you been hiding? I haven't heard from you in almost a year," said Chuck.

"I'm taking it slow. Went back to school," I said honestly. I do not volunteer that I am studying in a *yeshiva* unless someone asks me directly. Few people would understand. "Just wanted to know if you could have a look at a couple of hard disks for me."

"What's on them?"

"Right now? Nothing. The cyber guys at the East Lansing PD say they are clean. But I want you to tell me that they did not make a mistake," I said.

"I know Jackie Mills, that's their man," said Chuck. "We work together occasionally. He's good. If he says it's clean, it probably is. You'll be wasting your money."

"I still want it done," I insisted.

"Could take a look at the disks next week."

"No can do. They only gave me three days with the disks."

"I'm a little swamped right now. Big case going down and I'm getting all kinds of overtime."

"Big favor," I said beseechingly. "Gotta get this case wrapped up by the weekend."

The phone went silent for a moment and then Chuck said, "I'm really sorry. Can't do it before the weekend. I know we go way back."

"Yeah, way back to where I got them to drop your nephew's DUI."

"I remember."

"And your brother's aggravated assault."

"Yeah, that too."

"And the D&D charge for your Uncle Chet and ..."

"Yeah I remember all of those." He stopped speaking and then after a moment said reluctantly, "Can you drop off the disks this evening? I'll take a peek."

"My man!" I exclaimed. "Can't get them to you tonight. I'll drive back to Detroit tomorrow and bring you the disks."

"Where are you now?" Chuck asked.

"At the East Lansing Police station."

"That's your answer," he said excitedly.

"I told you they already checked the disks."

"Not Jackie," said Chuck. "You're gonna take your disks to the 'Disk Lady'. She works out of her home in East Lansing."

"No, Chuckie. Don't shunt me off. I need the best for this work," I insisted.

"Sy ... she is the best," he stated emphatically. "She's a living legend. There is no one better to check wiped disks. When we get stymied here in the division we sometimes farm out the disks to the 'Disk Lady'. She works with all the criminal justice systems in the state. DA, State Police, you name it."

"Can she be trusted?" I asked.

"Absolutely," he answered. "She is certified and bonded in all the fifty states to handle sensitive material. The FBI works with her. She even worked on some of the stuff you sent me last year and you didn't even know it. If you remember some of it was pretty nitty gritty."

Wow, what a revelation. If anything had leaked on some of those cases there could have been severe financial and political repercussions. "Thanks for telling me now," I said sarcastically.

"Hey, you want information off a computer, I get it for you. If it gets tough, I don't give up and sometimes I need special help. She's the special help."

"You think she'll take the disks on short notice?" I asked.

"I'm pretty sure she will. She works really crazy hours. I'll give her a call and tell her you're coming."

CHAPTER FOUR — The Vault

SLATTERLY BROUGHT ME THE disks, Chuck called back with the 'Disk Lady's' address and I arranged to meet with Julie Dalton the next morning. Then I took the file and disks to my car and when I punched 'Disk Lady's' address into the GPS, I found that she lived just one minute away from the station.

Should not take me long. I could get back to studying the file and maybe interview Rabbi Lipsky and the widow later in the day.

'Gypsy' was the pet name I have for the melodious voice of my GPS and when I am driving alone I sometimes have long conversations with her. She is a really good listener. Never argues. She only speaks up when she has something intelligent and important to say. So when Gypsy said I should turn right onto Elizabeth Street, a red light went on in my brain and I stopped the car. I started rummaging through the file and said, "What are you trying to tell me, Gypsy?"

It didn't take me long to find the answer.

Rabbi Klein's house was on Elizabeth Street. I punched his address into the GPS and found I was only three blocks away.

Things were looking even better. I could be home by tomorrow.

'Disk Lady' lived on Charles Street which was lined with one and two story wooden frame homes on big lots set way back from the street. None of the houses could be considered mansions but I figured they each had to have four or five bedrooms. Nice family places. All the homes seemed in good repair. The lawns were mowed and the shrubbery was clipped. Just about every house had bright flowering annuals blooming in planters, pots and highlighting the shrubbery. All in all, signs of a thriving neighborhood with lots of community pride.

Chuck told me 'Disk Lady's real name was Daphne La Claire. Not an unusual name for Michigan. One of the biggest lakes in the state was Lake St. Claire. There were still many descendents of the French Canadians that settled the area many generations ago. They were the ones that began the systematic screwing of the Potawatomi and Kickapoo Indians that had been the original occupants of this land. Once we white folk got our organized government up and running, the screwing of the Indians really got organized.

What an injustice.

It is easy to rationalize away all those atrocities because people like to forget.

In two hundred years I wonder what the world will remember of the Holocaust.

Daphne's house was a two story white trimmed grey colonial with shaped boxwood sentinel hedges guarding the front. Just in front of the greenery was a colorful mixture of daisies and begonias. The lawn needed mowing but had not reached the 'call the neighborhood vigilantes' stage. There were two children's bikes laying across the entrance walk. I could not tell if they were for girls or boys because the bikes nowadays have a unisex cross brace, but the pink handlebar streamers had me thinking girls. From the size of the bikes I would guess the kids were in the nine to twelve age range.

Am I a good detective, or what?

Let us see if I made any mistakes.

I rang the bell and opened the aluminum screen door. After a few moments I heard some voices, the white entrance door swung open and I was met by a slim, pretty teen age girl who appeared to be fourteen or fifteen and was wearing an oversized grey MSU sweatshirt and a dark blue pleated skirt. White scuffed gym shoes, no socks. Behind her black framed glasses I could see that her eyes were sky blue. Her long, straight, blonde hair was pulled back in a sloppy ponytail. Good looking kid.

So I was wrong about the age. I got the girl part right.

"Hi," I said in my most friendly tone.

Unless I am trying to purposefully intimidate someone, I almost always have to use my most friendly tone when I meet strangers. Over the years I have learned that people get a little frightened when they are suddenly confronted by an unknown six foot man standing on their doorstep. You also have to remember that I was decked out in my *yeshiva* black suit and fedora. That definitely was not an everyday sight for people in this neck of the woods. So, all in all, I was not one that was going to instill confidence in strangers. I cranked out my seven million dollar smile and added, "I'm Sy Lincoln and I'm looking for Daphne La Claire."

The girl looked me up and down, smiled and then out of the blue said, "That's me. *Shalom aleichem*. Chuck said you would be by."

Whammy!!!!!!

Double whammy!!!!!!

First of all. How did Chuck forget to tell me that Daphne is a child? How could I trust the disks to someone that was not much older than my niece?

Secondly, what was with the *shalom aleichem*? How did she know how to say that? Although there were over three thousand Jewish students at MSU the Jewish residents in the Greater Lansing area numbered only about one thousand. Considering there were almost half a million people living around here ... what were the odds? Those two words were the secret code of the Jewish nation. It was like a Western man caught in some God forsaken jungle and surrounded by primitive cannibals. As the natives approach menacingly, he thinks he is doomed. Then suddenly the chief comes forward, grabs his hand and gives him the secret Masonic handshake to show that they are brothers in the same sacred lodge. She just gave me the secret handshake. And she said it so well. Got the intonation perfect and the way she said the guttural "ch" sound shows she is no neophyte.

I could not believe that I just got the secret handshake.

Somehow I am able to stammer out the classic response of, "*Aleichem h'shalom*." Of course I am a long way from mastering the correct intonation and pronunciation, so what I say comes out sounding a pathetic, "*AH - lekem hasha - LOME*." Very pathetic.

My lame answer does not seem to faze her in the least.

"So what have you got for me?" she says holding out her hand to accept the disks.

What was I going to do? No way were the disks going into the hands of this teenager. I held up my hand and said, "Just one second. I have to make an important call. Be right back." I turned my back to Daphne and went back down to the street so that I had some distance between us.

I hit the speed dial for Chuck's number and at the second ring I heard him answer loudly, "Yo, talk to me."

"I'll talk to you all right," I said angrily in hushed whisper. "Why the hell didn't you tell me that the 'Disk Lady' is twelve years old?"

"Oh yeah, I forgot about that."

"How can you forget something like that?"

"Sy, she is not twelve years old," Chuck said trying to calm me.

"Oh she's not? What is she, eleven years old?" I answered testily.

"What I forgot to tell you is that she looks a lot younger than she is. I've worked with her for almost twelve years. She lived in Detroit before she moved to East Lansing. I think she's got a kid that's eleven or twelve years old."

I looked back at the girl who stood smiling smugly in the doorway. I wanted to be sure that I was not looking at Daphne's kid. I saw the fine crinkling of the skin at the corners of her eyes and the fullness around her mouth. Well ... yeah ... definitely not twelve years old.

Maybe … she was older than she looked.

I hesitated before I answered, "And she's good?"

"I'm telling you she's the best," said Chuck.

"If she screws this up I'm coming after you," I warned in jest.

"Never thought you wouldn't. You have nothing to worry about. If there is something on those disks, she'll find it," said Chuck emphatically.

"O.K., and thanks again," I said as I broke the connection and returned to the open door.

Before I could open my mouth she said, "And what did Chuck tell you?"

How the heck did she know who I had called? "How did you …?"

The girl finished my question, " … know you called Chuck? Easy. You can hear his 'Yo, talk to me' in the next county. Besides he's the one that sent you. So, what did he say?"

"About what?" I asked in mock innocence.

"What did he say when you asked him about how I looked too young to do your work?" she asked angrily.

"I didn't … I didn't …" I was able to stammer.

"Yes you did," she said placing her fists on her hips confronting me angrily. "Don't give me that denial crap. You were being judgemental. You are not the first person that thinks I look too young for serious work. Don't classify people or their capabilities by what they look like or set them in stereotypes." She stopped her tirade for a moment and then continued in a more subdued tone, "Judge people by their results. What they do. How they react. Not what they look like. You know what?" she said as she nodded her head making a mental decision. "I'm sick and tired of that bull. I think I'm not going to take your job. I don't need the work. Besides I think it is in very poor taste that you came to me in your '*yeshiva* boy' disguise. Which, by the way, doesn't work. So call Chuck and have him find you another disk magician. And, for your information ... and I have no idea why I'm telling you this ... on my next birthday I will be thirty one years old. Nice meeting you Mr. Lincoln," she said with finality and began to slam the door in my face.

Reflexively, my foot shot forward and I wedged my size twelve shoe between the door and the jamb before she could get it closed.

Fifteen years on the force taught me a few things. She was not going to slam the door in my face.

No siree.

But the move did not go as planned.

See, when I was on the force I wore heavy service shoes and there was little danger that my dainty foot would get crushed by a heavy door moving at a great velocity towards the door frame. But now I was wearing flimsy black gym shoes, because that's what you wore when you were in '*yeshiva* boy' mufti. Also it was a really heavy door and she was pushing for all she was worth.

Ouch!

That hurt.

I put on an even broader smile. I was not going to wince or show her I was in pain.

That was a macho rule. You toughed it out.

At first she could not figure out why the door would not close and was struggling to swing it shut. She looked out the door and saw my foot. Then she smiled and said mockingly, "Real smooth."

I tried to continue, "Look, Miss La Claire, I don't know ..."

Suddenly she yanked the door open again and said loudly, "My name is not La Claire. And my first name is not Daphne. My name is Dafna Lachler," she said in desperation. "Why can't you gentiles learn to say the 'ch' sound?"

"Because it's tough to do," I said in my defense. "You naturals don't know how tough it is. In order to make the 'ch' sound you got to move your tongue down towards the floor of your mouth and then make a sound that is somewhere between gargling, clearing your throat and choking to death. But I'm practicing."

"What are you practicing for ... Halloween?" she asked mockingly.

"In addition, Miss Lakler." That was as close as I could get to the 'ch' sound. "There is nothing wrong with being a gentile ... but as it happens ... I'm Jewish."

"It's Mrs. Lachler not Miss," she said. Then as she processed what I had just said her expression changed. She cocked her head to one side and sort of squinted, "You're Jewish?"

"Yes," I said proudly.

"Detective Sergeant Simon Lincoln of the Detroit Police Department. Tough street cop. Even tougher detective. Fifteen years on the force. Super tough private investigator. You're Jewish?" she asked incredulously.

How did she know all that information?

"What are you surprised about? Why can't I be Jewish? And what about you getting uppity and telling people that you don't even know not to be judgmental," I chided. "Seems to me it's the pot calling the kettle black."

She pointed her index finger at me and said, "No, it's not that. It's very rare to find Jewish cops. You see ..." she said tentatively. "I mean ... you do know? Over the years Jewish people have always gone for the free standing professions. You know doctors, lawyers, accountants. Mostly because they weren't allowed into the other professions. You could be the best darn farmer in the country but if the government decides to expel all the Jews you can't take your farm with you."

"But, I am Jewish, and I was a cop and now I am a private investigator." I hesitated for a moment and added, "Well, actually, right now I am not ... "

What was I trying to say?

"Not what, right now? Not Jewish? Not an investigator?" she asked.

"Never mind," I said waving my hand to stop this conversation. Why was I arguing with this lady? "I just want to know if you could check out my disks. If your answer is yes, fine. If not, I will be on my way. And what do you mean my 'yeshiva boy' disguise doesn't work. What's not to work about it?"

"Are you kidding me?" she asked adding a guffaw. "You're too old. Too big. And you say *'Aleichem h'shalom'* like you have just come back from communion. That's what doesn't work."

"Is that right?" I said nodding my head.

"Absolutely right. You will never be able to convince anyone with eyes and ears that you are a *Yeshiva* student," she said with finality.

"That's funny. See ... I have been learning in Rabbi Kalmonowitz's *Yeshiva* for the last eight months. So I guess that makes me a *yeshiva bocher*."

Dafna's mouth dropped opened, "You're kidding me."

I shook my head from side to side, "I'm afraid not. I am a *yeshiva bocher* ... *tzitzis* and all," I said holding out the fringes of my small prayer shawl that came out at the waist of my pants.

Dafna was still unable to speak. A female voice somewhere in the house yelled, "Daffy, what's keeping you?"

"Be right there, Mom. Someone's at the door," said Dafna still looking at me dumbfounded.

I heard a scamper of feet and then two girls dressed in long dresses stuck their small heads out the door. One was a blue eyed strawberry blonde who looked to be about twelve years old and she was accompanied by a dark haired ten year old. She also had blue eyes. The same color as Dafna. Most likely her daughters.

Bicycle mystery solved.

Am I the master of good efficient detective work and deduction, or what?

"Who's this?" asked the blonde.

The black haired girl looked me up and down and said, "Boy, you are very tall."

"These your kids?" I asked.

Dafna gained her composure and said, "None other. The big nosey one is Susie and the baby is Aliza."

The black haired girl said, "I am not a baby. I will be ten just before Rosh HaShana."

"I am sorry," said Mrs. Lachler. "This young lady is Aliza."

The young girl looked up at me and asked, "What's your name?"

"Simon Lincoln."

"Like the president?" asked Susie.

"Yeah, just like the president."

Aliza chimed in with, "Was he, like, your grandfather?"

"No, he wasn't," I answered simply.

"Girls stop pestering Mr. Lincoln," chided Dafna.

A short woman in her mid fifties, wearing a colorful house dress, came from deeper in the house. This was probably the mother.

Detective Lincoln making astounding deductions once again.

As the woman approached she said to Dafna and the girls, "What are you all doing standing in the doorway. That's not very polite." When she reached the door she saw me and looked me up and down. Then said appraisingly, "My, my, aren't you a big *yeshiva bocher*." She kept looking and added, "*Voos macht a yid*?"

This was another one of the secret handshakes of the Jewish people. It was phrase in Yiddish which literally meant something like 'How is a Jew doing?', but was much more complex. Say this phrase correctly to any other Jew and you were in. It was a combination of 'Hi, how are you?' and 'Even though I don't know you, can I be of any assistance to one of my Jewish brethren?'.

I had two problems with this phrase. First of all I as yet could not say it correctly. I was way off with the intonation and the second word had the impossible 'ch' sound. Secondly, Yiddish words and phrases were used all over the world — words like *nosherie, kibbitz, ganef, shmateh* and many more — and were so ubiquitous that I would not be surprised if the Archbishop of the Detroit diocese did not sprinkle them into his conversation. But I had never heard Yiddish spoken as a language until I reached the *yeshiva* and I still could not understand the most basic of sentences. Once, when someone hit me with the '*Voos macht a yid*' I answered with the stock expression of '*Baruch HaShem*' — a blessing be to God — meaning 'Thank God, I am doing all right'. The problem was, that when they heard my answer they just started speaking to me in rapid fire Yiddish and I was lost. So, to prevent any further misrepresentations, I let it be known right at the outset that I am a Yiddish boor.

I answered the woman, with, "I'm sorry. I don't speak Yiddish."

"That's OK, I don't know much myself. After '*Voos macht a yid*' I just coast," said the woman.

"This is my mother, Mrs. Kalin," said Dafna.

"What's with the Mrs. Kalin business? Call me Shaindel. Everyone does. That means beautiful in Yiddish, you know. In Hebrew my name is Yafah. Also means beautiful. Do you know that *yafah* is beautiful?" she asked me.

Yafah or *yafeh*, was one of the words I did know from my studies and I nodded my head and said, "Yes I do."

She looked at me and said knowingly, "I thought you would. Big handsome guy like you would know that *yafah* is beautiful."

Dafna was shocked and said, "Mom, what are you saying? You're embarrassing him."

Mrs. Kalin tilted her head and squinted just like Dafna had done, and said, "Are you married?"

Dafna blurted out, "Mom, what's the matter with you?"

Mrs. Kalin caught me off guard and before I could engage my brain, my mouth blurted out, "No, I'm single."

Where did that come from?

I had divorced Bethany over fourteen years earlier.

Good bye and good riddance.

So, I was indeed single.

Her mother quickly added, "That's good. That's very good. My daughter is available. She is a widow. She's dressed like a *shlump* — slob — right now so don't be judgmental. You should see her when she gets *farputzed*. She looks like a *malech*."

I had no idea what the word *farputzed* meant literally, but from the context I assumed it meant to get dressed up. *Malech* I knew was an angel. This was really cute, Mrs. Kalin was trying to set me up with her daughter.

Dafna yelled at her mother, "Mom, what are you doing?"

"What am I doing?" asked Mrs. Kalin rhetorically. "I'm trying to get you a date. You don't go out and you don't try."

"I'm fine the way it is," said Dafna defensively.

"But it is not fine the way it is," said Shaindel derisively. "Besides, why is he still standing on the doorstep? Is that polite? Invite him in." She turned to her granddaughters and asked, "What do I always say about guests at the door?"

Susie answered proudly, "If the person is not a stranger, you should never let them stand outside. Always invite them in."

Mrs. Kalin beamed, "See, I teach them good."

Aliza chimed in with an addition, "You told us, we should even invite in someone like nasty Mrs. Shaughnessy from across the street."

"Yeah, well, I guess I said that too," said Mrs. Kalin slightly embarrassed.

Dafna said, "I apologize for my mother's behavior. But she is right, please come in."

Shaindel turned to her granddaughters, "Girls come with me so that we can give Mr. Lincoln some privacy with your mom." She ushered the girls towards the back of the house and as she went she turned and gave me a big knowing wink.

Dafna pointed towards a flight of stairs, "Come let's go into 'The Vault'. That's where I work."

We went down about ten or twelve steps to reach the basement area. It looked just like most basements except for two things. To our right was an open doorway made of steel. The heavy steel door that sealed this opening was swung out into the basement and looked to be about twelve inches thick. It really was a vault.

What was this place?

The second unusual feature was a huge tank with dials and levers that sat to the left of the door. It went from floor to ceiling and back about fifteen feet. I turned to Dafna, pointed to the tank and asked, "What is that?"

She glanced at the tank and said, "Come in first, I'll explain in a moment." She went through the opening and swept her arms in a wide arc, "This is where I work. My kingdom."

The huge room had a ten foot high ceiling and was an oblong forty feet deep and thirty feet wide. Using the front of the house as my point of orientation, I figured that this whole room extended out of the basement into the backyard. There were large cabinets that went from floor to ceiling on either side of the entrance. The other three walls had a continuous desk/shelf that ran around the room and above this desk were two and three tier banks of computer screens that also went around the room. About half of the computer screens were active. In the center there was an island that held a variety of machines and contraptions. There was a workshop area that held some machines that I recognized, like a drill press and a table saw. But there were other machines that were a complete mystery. There was one large item that was basically a large framed glass box with a number of openings. Sealed to these openings were large rubber gloves. Something dangerous or intricate was done in that box, but I had no idea what it could be. The room was brightly illuminated by LED lights fitted into the ceiling. Since we were under ground level there were obviously no windows but a number of air conditioning vents kept the room comfortable.

Pretty impressive layout.

"You built this room?" I asked.

"You mean 'The Vault'? No way. Nowadays it would cost maybe one hundred grand to build ... maybe more. It's got reinforced concrete walls and look at the size of it. The roof is two feet thick and doubles as an outdoor patio for the backyard. This room was the reason I bought this place when we moved here from Detroit," said Dafna.

"Chuck told me you were from Detroit."

"Still have the house there and it has a room just like this one. We rent it out, although at the moment we are between tenants."

"Was the previous owner of this house also a computer nut?" I asked.

"No, all the computer stuff is mine. The previous owner was a 'prepper' until the day he died at age eighty eight. This place was filled with shelves from floor to ceiling loaded with tons of food and material, all ready for the end of the world. Boy was he surprised when he passed and found that no one had dropped a bomb on him and all his stuff remained unused. That tank that you saw outside is a commercial liquid propane container and was supposed to give him a five year supply of gas."

"Is that legal in a residence?"

"Totally illegal. To get around the zoning rules he dug a pit outside with concrete walls and floor. Then he had the tank installed. Once he had it filled with propane he broke out the basement wall so that the tank was now connected with the cellar. Then he built a concrete roof over the pit because if push ever came to shove, then ... "

"Push to shove?" I asked.

"Armageddon Day. That's what all the preppers are preparing for," she said stating the obvious. "He did not want his neighbors to have any way of getting at his propane. When we first moved in we had a gas guy out here to see about removing the tank. He said it would involve a crane and police and permits and we would also have to shell out $7,000 in demolition and reconstruction costs. He told us off the record that if it was his propane tank, he would simply use the gas until it empties the tank. So that is what we have been doing. He comes out every six months and inspects the integrity of the tank. Apparently it held a lot more than he thought because so far we have used the gas for six years. He thinks we are getting down to the last of it, but can't be sure because when it gets toward the end, the gauges are not entirely accurate. Maybe six months ... maybe less."

"Still a six month supply of gas sitting under the house? That sounds like a time bomb ready to explode."

Dafna shook her head, "The gas guy says these tanks are used in factories all over the place and experience shows that they are perfectly safe."

"Unless you have a house fire, or an electrical short or lightning strikes ... Need I say more?"

"Thank you , Mr. Grim," said Dafna with a mocking smile. "The propane guy says those things would not ignite the gas. You would need some sort of explosion to breach the integrity of the tank. Anyway, when we were looking for a house, this huge concrete storeroom made the sale. I knew it would be perfect for my business."

Who is the 'we' that was looking for a house?

"You and your mom bought this house?" I asked.

Dafna turned solemn, "No, me and my husband. He came to study here. David passed away two years ago. Cancer."

"I'm so sorry," I said.

"What are you sorry for? You were not responsible ... that was God's doing."

"It must have been tough," I offered lamely.

"It was," she said nodding her head sadly. "I've still got a score to settle with him."

"With your husband?"

"No," she said. "With God."

She stopped speaking and was contemplating who knows what. I did not attempt to break into her thoughts. When it became a little more than awkward I cleared my throat and she looked up.

"Oh yeah. Your disks. I have got to decide if I will work with you."

"Is there a problem?"

"No problem," she said with a knowing smile. "Do you know what my business is?"

"You check disks for the police and other law enforcement agencies," I ventured.

"Wrong," she said emphatically. "That's my hobby. It makes up less than one percent of my income. What I do to make money, ninety nine percent of the time is resurrect disks. You accidentally erase your disk, your disk fails mechanically, you run your disk through the washing machine, have an elephant step on your disk or you just plain lose your data ... you come to me. I am able to restore over ninety percent of lost data for businesses and private customers. That's how I make my living. If I relied only on the law enforcement groups I would starve to death. Also it takes a lot of time and the agencies don't pay that well. So, why do I do work with the police? Because resurrecting disks is boring as hell. Don't tell my mother I said 'hell'. Working for the agencies is fun. That's why I do it."

"But isn't it the same work?" I asked.

"No way," she said. "Every disk I get from the police is a mystery and I am a mystery freak. I read every new mystery book that comes out. I'm a platinum customer of the Amazon and Barnes & Noble mystery book clubs. It's my one great passion and my only real pleasure. So when I get a police disk, I drop whatever I am doing and solve the mystery placed before me."

"So you will take my disks?"

"Not so fast," she said holding up her palm. "I have a question."

"You know I can't reveal any information about my investigation."

"Fair enough," she said. "I'll just ask one question. Is this investigation in the Greater Lansing area?"

"Well, that I can answer," I said with a nod. "Yes, it is in this area."

"Great!" she said with a yelp. "Here's the deal. I will check your disks for you on the condition that you allow me to help you with this investigation."

How did this happen? I can't let just anyone be part of an investigation. I will lose my license. "I don't think so ..."

"What's the problem? I won't get in your way. I've been dreaming about being involved with a real life investigation for as long as I can remember," she said with enthusiasm. "But nothing ever happens in East Lansing. Finally, I have my opportunity."

"But there is personal information involved and I am not allowed to reveal such material," I said with determination.

"What are you nuts?" she chided. "Once you give me the disks I will know just about everything there is to know about the people under investigation. You are forgetting that I handle sensitive material all the time and I am certified and bonded to do just that. Isn't there some sort of form I can sign that makes me an assistant or something? Then there should be no problem. Besides I know the Greater Lansing area and you don't."

The lady knows her stuff. She was absolutely correct. If we have a contract of even one dollar then she officially would be my employee. Part of my staff. I would have no ethical problems. "I don't know," I said stalling.

"I'll tell you what. If you let me help you, I do the disks for free," she said earnestly. "That's a good deal. I usually take $300 for every hour of my time and another $50 an hour for the time my computer is chewing though the disk. We're talking a $500 up to a $3,000 discount and maybe more. What do you say?"

"I still don't think that ..."

"Bottom line," she said with finality. "Either you take my deal and we are partners on this case ... or you can take your disks elsewhere."

I don't believe this. I am being blackmailed by a little nutsy computer lady. I quickly assessed my options.

I had no options.

There really was no one I knew that was available in the next three days and had the savvy to adequately check disks that the police say were clean. I could simply assume that the East Lansing cops were correct and write off the disks, but that was not my way. I had to check every angle. If I didn't, I knew it would haunt me forever.

What was the downside if she worked with me? She would already know everything about Rabbi Klein the moment she looked at the disks. The case looked to be an open and shut suicide, so there was no real danger for either of us.

After a moment I asked, "Didn't your mother ever teach you what she taught your daughters, to never let a stranger into your house?"

"Sure she did."

"So, why are you so eager to become my assistant in this investigation," I questioned. "I'm a stranger. You don't know me at all."

She suddenly smiled and said, "You're no stranger. You're Simon Lincoln. Age thirty seven. Born and raised in Bloomfield Hills. Spent two years in the Marines, and after your discharge — technically an honorary discharge — you went to the Detroit Metropolitan Police Academy." She stopped and squinted at me again, "By the way what was that strange discharge? Did something happen?"

That had been a very traumatic time in my emotional life. I had no intention of sharing all the details with this woman, "Nothing that you need to know."

She looked at me funny and then continued, "You were a cop for fifteen years and worked your way up to detective sergeant. About three years ago you were involved in a shooting incident. You killed the perpetrator but got shot in the process. Three months later, when you came back from your medical leave, you resigned. Since then you got yourself a PI license and have been running 'Lincoln Investigations' based in Warren, Michigan. You look just like your picture but until I saw you in the flesh, I didn't realize just how tall you were. About the only surprise is that I did not know you were now in a *Yeshiva*."

Where in the world did she get this information? She had to have hacked into the records of the police department. I waggled a finger at her and said, "I should call the cops and have you arrested."

"Me arrested? For what?" she asked innocently.

"For computer fraud or infringement or whatever. There is no way that you could have gotten that information legally. You belong in jail," I warned.

"What information are you talking about?" she asked coyly.

"What you just told me. My entire biography. That's what."

"Me? You must be mistaken. You are a stranger. You just came to the door. How could I know anything about you?" she asked logically. "I think you must be confusing me with someone else."

Smooth. She just denies everything and I have nothing to prove she hacked into my most personal information. "Why do you want to work with me? So far this case looks like it is open and shut. I am just going to interview the people involved and tie up any loose ends. I doubt there will be any major revelations. Most likely it will just be grunge detective work. You are going to be bored out of your skull."

"See ... you just said it ... it's a simple case. I won't be a bother. It can't be any more boring than watching a disk go round and round," she said holding her hands together in supplication. "Please, please, please, please and pretty please," she begged.

My mind must have turned to oatmeal mush. I could not think of a good argument to fend her off. In a moment of weakness I found myself nodding and saying, "OK, but you have to follow my lead and obey whatever I tell you to do. As of this moment we have an official verbal agreement that you are in my employ." I pulled a dollar from my bill fold and handed it to her, "Here is your salary."

Dafna took the dollar and then punched her fist in the air as she yelled, "Yes!"

"And, we are not partners ... you are my assistant. If I think there is any danger, you are out. And I want the information of the disks ASAP."

"Give me those disks."

I handed her the plastic bag and she quickly attached electrical cords to the disks. She sat before a computer terminal and her fingers floating over the keys as she started up some program. Numbers and signs ran across the computer screen.

After about ten minutes, she swung around in her chair and asked, "You want the good news or the bad news first?"

"I don't know ... just make it so it doesn't hurt too much."

"The bad news is that on the initial assessment, it looks like both the disks are complete with no deliberate erasures or hiding of files. So Jackie Mills was right in his evaluation. Nothing on the disks."

"What's the good news?" I asked skeptically.

"The good news is, I think he missed a 'Google Swipe' on the laptop disk," she stated with a smirk.

OK, I'll bite.

"What's a 'Google Swipe'?" I asked.

"Do you really want to know?" asked Dafna nodding her head in warning.

She was right. Even if I knew what it meant it wouldn't make a difference. "Why don't you give me an idiot's introduction to a 'Google Swipe'. I figure that will be more than enough."

"A 'Google Swipe' is what I call it when someone uses one of the programs that pop up when you ask Google how to secretly erase files from your disk so no one knows," she explained.

"Isn't that an oxymoron or something?" I questioned. "If the program works, then how can you know they did a 'Google Swipe'?"

She considered her words before answering, "I just can."

"And other computer gurus can't?"

Again she hesitated before answering, "No, they can't."

"So, you can find the files?"

"I can find which files were erased with the swipe. But right now I have no idea what they contain. It might have nothing to do with your case. The disks are being processed as we speak," she said.

"How much time?" I asked concerned.

"My guess is between twenty-four and thirty-six hours until we have results."

"Can't you speed it up?" I beseeched.

"Big negative to that. It's a long complicated decryption and these are just about the fastest computers. Twenty-four to thirty-six hours is about right."

"Darn it," I said.

"No, this is good. We will have enough time to solve the mystery together," she said with a smile.

"I almost forgot."

"But I did not," she said wagging her index finger at me. "Partner, it is time we got started. Let's go to the kitchen to get some coffee and you can fill me in."

"You are my assistant … not my partner," I corrected.

"Whatever," was all she said as she marched out of the Vault.

I had no choice but to follow.

CHAPTER FIVE — Whammy

I FOUND CLIMBING THE STAIRS behind Dafna Lachler to be ... for want of a better term ... captivating, because apparently I had subliminally switched from *yeshiva bocher* mode into healthy normal male mode. I automatically began appreciating her long graceful neck, her shapely swaying butt, and her curvy legs. Not bad at all.

'Shame on me', I thought. That is not the way a *yeshiva bocher* should look at women. Actually, he probably should not look at women at all.

But, I was on an investigatory mission for Rabbi Kalmonowitz. I am only investigating. I just have to clean up my act.

Dafna turned her head around as she walked and asked, "What kind of coffee do you like? We got one of those snazzy coffee machines ... with the pods. You know George Clooney stuff. Maybe you'd like a piece of my mother's cake?"

Now it becomes awkward.

One of the most difficult parts of being a *yeshiva bocher* is dealing with other people's conception of my kosher dietary restrictions. This included non-religious Jews. I could not eat anything that was not 100% kosher. That meant I had to have kosher ingredients and they had to be cooked and served in kosher utensils with strict separation of milk and meat dishes. Just because Dafna's mom could say '*Voos macht a yid*', did not certify her homemade cake as kosher.

It was always embarrassing to refuse a host's proffered food.

We were just passing through the living room/den area and I scanned the layout. The room looked clean and tidy. The high bookshelves were crammed with books and blended well with the comfortable looking sofas and chairs. Very homey. Very nice.

My mind suddenly clicked into overdrive.

Why did this room look so homey and nice?

I stopped walking and scrutinized the room more closely. It only took a moment to digest what I had seen but not processed when I first saw the room.

Dafna turned back from the kitchen door, "Is there something wrong?"

Whammy!!!! Triple Whammy!!!!

The floor to ceiling shelves covered almost an entire wall and the reason the room looked so homey was because almost all the books were written in Hebrew. There was a set of the Talmud, of Maimonides, the bible and more and more. Hundreds of scholarly books. How had I missed it?

Easy.

As an older and single *yeshiva bocher* I was invited for *Shabbos* meals to the homes of the married *bocherim* and rabbis. I saw their home libraries. Some could afford more books and some less, but they all had some sort of library at home. A simple God fearing observant Jew might have a few basic books at home. A less observant one maybe just a bible and his prayer books for the week and High Holidays. Few had libraries as extensive as what I was seeing in Dafna's living room. This was exactly like the warm comfortable homes that I had frequented for the past eight months.

I assume that the books had belonged to her husband. That meant he had to be one serious Torah student — a *talmid chacham* — and an observant Orthodox Jew. He could even have been a rabbi. That meant that Dafna was an observant Orthodox Jew living way out here in East Lansing.

What were the odds?

In twenty minutes Daphne La Claire had gone from being a French Canadian *shiksa* to Dafna Lachler, American *Rebbitzen*.

Quadruple Whammy!!!!

She said again, "Is there something wrong. You're standing there like a statue."

I suspect I had been frozen there with my mouth wide open, because I consciously felt how my lips came together. I turned to Dafna, "You're *frum* — religious."

"Yeah, we are. Is that a crime in Michigan?"

"If you're Orthodox Jewish ... here in East Lansing ..." I said thinking out loud. "That has got to mean that you are connected with Rabbi Lipsky's *kollel*."

"Brilliant deduction. You know, you should think about becoming a detective," she said sarcastically.

"So are you connected?"

"Well, of course, we were. Up until my husband's death he learned in the *kollel*. When he passed away they brought in another family. But we still go there on *Shabbos*. It's a really small community. Fifteen Orthodox families for all of the Greater Lansing area."

Did this change anything? She knew the people involved in the case. Was this good or bad?

"Mrs. Lachler, ..."

"Call me Dafna. Mrs. Lachler is my mother-in-law."

"Dafna ... we have a problem. The case I'm working on ..."

"Yeah? What about it," she asked suspiciously. "Are you trying to weasel out of our deal?"

I raised my eyebrows and shook my head, "No, I'm not ... it's just that the case I'm investigating is Rabbi Klein's suicide."

Her facial expression became serious, "Holy Cow! Does this mean that someone thinks he did not kill himself?"

"Well, yeah," I said stating the obvious.

"Who hired you? Who thinks someone did something to Rabbi Klein?" she asked eagerly.

Could I tell her? What could it hurt?

"First of all ... remember you are my assistant. You cannot tell a soul," I scolded.

"Yeah, yeah. I tell no one. Who hired you?" her interest was piqued to the extreme.

"I was hired by ..." I stopped speaking for a moment just to torment her. " ... by Rabbi Kalmonowitz."

"I knew it. I knew it. It had to be *Rebbi*," she said enthusiastically. "You know, he sees things. He feels and sees things that you and I do not. If he thinks there was foul play here ... you can take it to the bank."

"All the evidence points to a routine suicide. Everything was checked and there was nothing suspicious," I said firmly.

"And did you not hear what I said? You can take it to the bank," she said determinedly. "Fill me in on what you know."

"That's the problem, Dafna. I can't just yet," I said as she looked at me inquisitively. "I just found out that you are a little too close to this case. I want to talk with Rabbi Lipsky and get his approval first."

"Is that all?" she said with a shrug. She stuck her head into the kitchen and said, "Mom, I'm going out for a bit with Mr. Lincoln."

I heard Mrs. Kalin respond loudly, "That's nice. Have a good time. Let me know when a Mazel Tov is in order."

"Mom, for God's sake. Stop already," said an exasperated Dafna. Then she turned, grabbed her purse and car keys and headed for the door but not before she said over her shoulder to me, "Why are you standing there like a *Golem*? We have to get Rabbi Lipsky's approval."

CHAPTER SIX — Kollel

THE RABBI, HIS WIFE and eight kids, apparently lived on the second floor and part of the attic, of a large house just off Elizabeth Street. At present, he had only four kids living at home — the others were off learning in *yeshivas* — so for now they were not too crowded. The ground floor was the home of the Greater Lansing Area *Kollel* and was basically just a large space with doors leading out to a small kitchen and washroom. This main room was a combination synagogue/study-hall/meeting room. The place was just a few blocks from Dafna Lachler's home, but this was to be expected. The community had to be geographically compact, because it was forbidden to use vehicles on the Sabbath and *frum* people would have to walk to the synagogue, so the distances could not be great.

There were two pairs of *bocherim* learning at the half dozen tables in the book-lined study hall. Rabbi Lipsky was in his shirt-sleeves, up on a ladder on the east wall of the room, trying to repair the rope pull that opened the decorative curtain in front of the Holy Ark. The ark contained the Torah scroll and was the 'holiest' item in the synagogue. The Jews are called the 'People of the Book' — The Torah Scroll is 'The Book'. The rabbi wore a black skull cap and was about forty five years old. He was of average height and weight and had a wispy salt and pepper beard. I walked into the room but Dafna stayed at the door. I turned back to her and asked, "Why don't you come in?"

"I can't," she said in frustration. "There are men learning in there. It would be improper."

She was absolutely right. I was only twelve hours out of the *bais medrash* and I was already forgetting *frum* world etiquette. Women did not walk around the *bais medrash* if men were present. Understanding the problem, I said, "Wait here, I'll get Rabbi Lipsky."

I walked up to the rabbi and introduced myself and explained the reason for my visit. He immediately came down the ladder and directed us both towards his domicile on the second floor.

As we climbed the stairs the rabbi said, "I'm glad you came just now. I have no idea how to fix that cord. If I kept up I was going to totally break the whole *gesheft*."

Once again I had no idea what the word *gesheft* meant but I guess it had something to do with the mechanism or something. The rabbi went up first, I followed and as per etiquette, Dafna came last.

As we entered his home he yelled out, "Chanah, look who's here."

I assumed Chanah was his wife and after a moment a rotund woman wearing a *tichel* — head scarf — came out of the kitchen wiping her hands on her apron. She took one look at Dafna and smiled, "Dafnaleh, good to see you in the middle of the week."

"You know how busy I get," said Dafna in her defense.

"Don't I know it," said Chanah with a smile. She looked at me and said, "She's a real *aishess chayil*."

I knew that expression. An *aishess chayil* was a woman of valor. More important, a woman that made a good living, so that her *Yeshiva* boy husband could sit and learn. An *aishess chayil* was a commodity very much in demand in the *yeshiva* world.

I turned to *Rebbitzen* Lipsky and said in mock seriousness, "Thank you for letting me know that. That is very important information." How interesting. Everyone was trying to make a match for Dafna.

I could feel Dafna staring daggers at my back.

I suppose happily married couples develop something like telepathy or clairvoyance and are able to understand one another without a word being spoken. I never had anything like that with my ex ... we had more like an anti-telepathy. But the Lipskys seem to have it, because the *rebbitzen* came over and said, "Dafnaleh, why don't you come with me for a moment, so we can give the men time to talk."

Somehow, Chanah knew that her husband wanted to speak to me in private.

Even though I had only met Dafna the hour before, I intuitively knew that going with *Rebbitzen* Lipsky was just about the last thing she wanted to do. Still it was necessary that I talk to the rabbi and if she was in the room it would complicate everything, "Dafna, I think that would be a good idea. I have to get Rabbi Lipsky's approval of my plans ... if you know what I mean."

I could see Dafna resign herself to the inevitable and left the room with the *rebbitzen*.

When we were alone Rabbi Lipsky turned to me and said seriously, "Rabbi Kalmonowitz spoke with me. I don't know what surprised me more. That Rabbi Klein took his own life or that Rabbi Kalmonowitz thinks he did not."

"I can imagine it must be quite a shock."

"I understand from Rabbi Kalmonowitz that you are a private investigator. Strange combination, private investigator — *yeshiva bocher*."

"You don't know how strange," I said with a smile. Then I put on my serious face and asked, "So, what do you think happened?"

"Me? What do I know? If you would have told me that Avraham Klein was someone that could take his own life I would have told you that you are crazy," he said with determination. "Rabbi Klein was the one who could talk just about anyone out of committing suicide. I know, because he counseled disturbed students from the university."

It was hard to imagine a typical college student feeling comfortable in the *Kollel*. "Did he talk with them here?"

"No, definitely not here," said the rabbi. "I assume it was somewhere on campus or the Hillel House, but I don't know where."

"So, you think it was not suicide."

"Who knows what is in another man's heart? Only the *Kodesh Baruch Hoo* — God," said the rabbi nodding his head. "About five weeks ago, out of the blue, Rabbi Klein told me that for personal reasons he would have to leave his position as head of the *kollel*. When I tried to pin him down, he refused to tell me his reasons. He did say that it would probably be for at least one half year, maybe more. He liked his work here in the *kollel* but would understand if I could not keep his job open for him."

"Was he upset when he said this?" I asked.

"No," said the rabbi recalling the conversation. "He was as cool as a cucumber."

I started asking the stock questions you ask when you are investigating a death. "Did he have any enemies? Were there any financial or business difficulties? Did any of the students he counseled suffer from psychiatric problems? Did he suffer from any psychiatric or physical problems?"

"The police here in East Lansing asked me all those questions and I understand why you have to ask them, but the answer is no to all of them. We all loved Avraham Klein and I am sure he knew it. I can't think of a soul who would want to hurt him," said the rabbi lapsing into silence. After a moment, "In answer to your first question — No, I don't think Avraham Klein committed suicide. But I don't know who killed him or how they could have done it."

From his statement I understood that he had some knowledge of the circumstances and facts of the case. He, therefore, must know that the evidence indicated that Rabbi Klein had been alone in his house when he died and that there were no signs of foul play. The question was, how did he know? The police shared the information with me because they were giving me cooperation up the whazoo, but why should the local rabbi have that information? Simplest way to find out is ask. "How do you know about how he died?"

"From *Rebbitzen* Klein," he said simply. "The police reported to her about what they had found and she told me. Is there something wrong?"

Nothing really wrong with that. Good police community relations. Still, it was a bit early to allow public access to all the information. "No problem," I said with a smile. "Just wanted to know."

"Just think ... finding your husband hanging in the basement ... I can't imagine what it must have been like for Devorah," said the rabbi shaking his head.

"Did the rabbi get along with his wife?"

"Devorah? They were like love birds. Kosher love birds, of course," he said emphatically. "She took care of everything that was related to the house. Their home was always like a showplace. And her meals ... she can cook like a dream. Don't tell Chanah I said that. Everywhere they went they went together. Like I said ... Kosher love birds. It was a shame they could never have children."

"Did *Rebbitzen* Klein have a physical problem that prevented her from having children?"

"I have no idea. Maybe my wife knows something, but as you can imagine it was not a subject for open discussion."

I had to clarify a point that bothered me from the outset, "You said they always went everywhere together. So how is it that *Rebbitzen* Klein went to the movies, all on her own, every Wednesday evening? From what I know about the *frum* community most *Rebbitzen*s would not go to see films at all."

"You're right," said the rabbi with a nod. "Except this was Devorah's one weakness. She loved films. Always had. *Reb* Avraham told her he would never go to a movie theater and he also told her that he felt that it was not appropriate for her as well. But Devorah was a very determined woman. They finally came to an agreement that she would go to the last show at the theater, so that very few people would see her."

There are all sorts of determined women in this world and it was crucial in this case to know what kind of determined woman *Rebbitzen* Klein was. "Let me see if I got this straight. He said 'No'. She said 'Yes'. And the agreement reached was 'Yes'. Nice compromise. Is she that kind of determined woman?"

From the look on the rabbi's face I could see he understood my question and he said, "You've got it exactly. She is a determined woman."

"And if she doesn't get her way ... what happens?" I asked.

"Then she becomes an even more determined woman," he said with a knowing nod.

"I see," I said. Good to be warned about problematic personalities. "I have a small difficulty that needs your assistance."

"Whatever it is, you got it."

"I need Dafna Lachler's help to check the computer disks from the Klein home but she is blackmailing me. Unless I let her help me on the case she won't get me the information on the disks."

"Is that allowed?" he asked.

"You mean blackmailing me?"

"No ... for someone like her to work on an investigation?"

"Yes and no ... I mean yes ... but it's complicated. That's not the problem," I said dismissingly. "The difficulty is that she knows the people involved. Will this be a problem? Will it cloud her judgment? Will it interfere with the investigation?"

"What does this have to do with me?"

"I want your approval to allow her to work with me," I said simply.

"Now you have put me in a difficult situation," said the rabbi.

"How so?"

"Do you know how this *kollel* works?" asked the rabbi.

Typical Jewish answer. Answer a question with a question. "I suppose it is a Jewish study hall."

"Absolutely right, but it is much much more," said Rabbi Lipsky. "Seven years ago I was approached by a dozen Jews living here in the Greater Lansing area. They told me that although there was an active Hillel House just off campus, it was geared for the students and not families. There are Conservative and Reform Temples here but the nearest regular Orthodox synagogue is over fifty miles away. They wanted a real house of prayer. A place to bring their children to gain an insight into Jewish values. They purchased this house and offered to pay a rabbi's salary for five years. I explained to them that without a daily *minyan* it would be impossible to have an Orthodox synagogue."

"Why would that prevent you from opening a synagogue?" I asked.

"If there was no daily *minyan* it would just be an empty building, with no impact on the community," said the rabbi.

"I see."

"So, since they could not guarantee that ten local Jews would be available three times a day, we came up with the idea of the *kollel*. This serves two purposes. First, with six *kollel* students, the *kollel* rabbi and me, we had eight. We figured that we would be able to recruit two more Jews to fill the required number on a voluntary rotational basis. The *bocherim* are officially here from seven in the morning to ten at night every day except *Shabbos* — European pronunciation of *Shabbat*. Besides their self-learning these *bocherim* get lessons from the *kollel* rabbi and some guest rabbis from the Detroit *yeshivas*. On top of all that, I also run an outreach program and I require that each one of the *bocherim* teach Torah to anyone that wants to learn. So they all give classes to groups and individuals, here and at their homes."

"What does this have to do with Dafna?" I asked.

"I'm getting to that," said Rabbi Lipsky. "As with many synagogues, our biggest problem is money. The more successful we are ... meaning when more people come to our services and *Shabbos* meals, we go deeper into the hole. The people that started this place have been extremely generous, but for the day to day running of the *shul* we have to rely on donations. The problem is that most of our customers for the services and the meals are from the transient student population and for the most part they haven't got a dime. The *kollel* students are all married and require salaries so that their families have a roof over their heads and food on the table. The money collected from their teaching is not enough." The rabbi stopped speaking and looked at me directly.

I realized that he wanted me to reach a logical conclusion from what he said so far. But what did this have to do with Dafna?

I got it.

"And that is where Dafna fits in."

"Bingo," said the rabbi pointing his index finger at me. "Dafna has a good business. I don't really know what it is, but you already said it has something to do with computer disks. She is one of many *frum* people that give a tithe — ten percent — of their yearly profits to charity. She has a really good business."

"And she is one of your benefactors," I said with a knowing nod.

"Bingo again," said the rabbi.

"And you can't say anything against her because she might stop donating to the *kollel*," I said stating the logical assumption.

"Now, don't get me wrong," said the rabbi shaking his palms in front of my face. "I cannot believe that if for some reason I said that you should not work with Dafna that she would stop her donations. Actually, the opposite is true. Dafna is a real *neshama* — someone with a soul. She knows everyone and everyone knows her, and you won't find a single person who will say one bad word about her. Her husband, David, *alav ha'shalom* — May his soul find peace — was one of the first *bocherim* in the *kollel*. He never took a salary. Not a penny. She supported him and raised their two daughters and kept a beautiful home and gave donations to the *kollel*. She is also as smart as a whip and a fountain of knowledge in

Torah and secular subjects. I think she could rival our best *bocher* if she set her mind to it."

"So, as far as her working with me … do you approve or don't you approve?" I asked.

"Oh, I approve. Definitely approve," said the rabbi with a smile.

CHAPTER SEVEN — Pinball Pete's

So, I WAS NOW temporarily partnered with Mrs. Dafna Lachler. Well, not partners ... I was the boss. She was subservient to me. Those were the rules.

Question is ... does she know it?

I had left my car at her house so we were sitting in her Chrysler van outside the *kollel*. I was filling her in with the basic facts of what I had learned from Jumpin' Jack and Rabbi Lipsky.

I could not get over how eager and excited she was.

When you see a small dog there never is a problem of confusing it with a young puppy. That's because the puppy behaves in such a unique way ... always prancing about and moving with jerky movements. It is constantly exploring and learning and it does it all with an eager enthusiasm.

That was Dafna, but without the prancing and jerky movements.

She wanted to look through the case file immediately but I insisted that I wanted to see it first. She could have a look at it tomorrow.

The next step in the investigation could get awkward. I needed to set up a meeting with *Rebbitzen* Klein and hopefully get a look at the 'scene of the crime'. That meant I had to get into her house. Problem was, it was not acceptable for a man to meet alone with a religious woman at her home. Dafna surprised me by intuitively recognizing the difficulties in meeting with the *rebbitzen* and suggested that she make the arrangements to meet with her. That way, I would just be tagging along.

Good idea.

She called the *rebbitzen* but the woman said she would be out of her home until late afternoon. Dafna set up a meeting at her house at 5:30 pm.

We had two hours to kill, "What do people in East Lansing do for fun?"

"I have no firsthand experience, but from what I understand, most people in this area either hunt, fish, or drink" said Dafna. "I am not sure in what order."

That made me laugh, "Yeah, that's probably true for most of rural USA."

"You want to see something special ... right around here?" she said eagerly.

"Sure, I'm game."

She drove her car to the corner of M.A.C. Avenue and Albert. I recognized the street and realized that we were just about a block south of the police station and one block north of the MSU campus. We parked in a lot behind a small strip mall and when we came around the building I saw an ostentatious neon sign that said, 'Pinball Pete's'.

"What is this place?" I asked.

"My girls love it," she said with a smile. "It's an old fashioned penny arcade."

The place was long and narrow with game machines crammed along the sides and up two rows in the middle. Thin strips of fluorescent lights shone from the ceiling but most of the room's illumination came from the colored lights on the front panels of the machines. There was a cashier's booth just to the right of the door where you could change bills into quarters ... the coin needed to make all the magic happen. The place was not all that big and there were only about a dozen people scattered around the emporium playing a variety of games. Most of the games were variations of the classic pinball machines but there were also, skee bowl lanes, air hockey, an old fashioned mechanical gypsy to tell your fortune, and much, much, more.

From the look on Dafna's face I could tell that it was not just her daughters who liked the place. I changed a twenty into quarters and we went around feeding the machines and making the magic happen.

Dafna was enjoying herself. She had a cute smile and an even cuter laugh.

Hey, slow down, *yeshiva bocher*. You are not supposed to notice such things.

Wait a second ... I am on a break from the *yeshiva*, and investigators are allowed to make such observations. Part of the job. Good detective work.

I knew I was kidding myself, but I was also having a good time.

I had to admit that after my monastic eight months, it was fun to be in the company of someone of the female persuasion.

I was shooting an electronic rifle at the mechanical bears that were audaciously crossing the painted scenery, when Dafna stated, "I saw in your records that you were married once."

There she was again with my personal information — "You mean the records you have never ever seen?"

"Yeah, those records," she said smiling. After a pause she asked softly, "What happened?"

Now, that is super personal, but the way she asked the question — with such real empathy — she made me feel comfortable enough to answer, "We both were too young, too impetuous, too stupid. We never should have married. It was just one unending argument that last year together. We did both of us a favor when we got divorced."

"Any children?"

"Thank God, no," I said with relief.

"Was she Jewish?"

That was a question from left field.

I don't know why, but her honest concern made me feel that I could tell her things that I had never said aloud to anyone.

I shot two bears and heard them roar.

Then I rested the rifle in the crook of my arm and said, "Bethany was not Jewish, but when you look at all the facts, I suppose I was not Jewish either. Oh, my parents were both born and raised in Jewish homes but they were never really religious."

"Didn't you have any kind of *yiddishkeit* — Jewish culture — in your life?" she asked sympathetically.

"I'm not sure I really know what 'Yiddish quite' is," I answered.

"Some kind of exposure to your Jewish cultural heritage. Did you have a *Bar Mitzvah*?"

"Oh yeah, come to think of it, I did," I said remembering back twenty-four years. "One Friday night my dad took us all to the temple in Bloomfield Hills. I can still visualize him passing a check to the rabbi. Then the assistant rabbi — a woman — had us all stand up at the front of the temple. We were about six boys and maybe half as many girls. She said a whole bunch of stuff out loud and had us repeat after her. Might have been *brochas* — blessings — or the *Shema*, but I can't remember. I do know that I had no idea what I was saying. The head rabbi, a balding guy, gave a twenty minute boring speech. And that was it. My *Bar Mitzvah*."

"You didn't have a special dinner or party?" inquired Dafna.

"My family went out for a celebratory dinner of ribs and lobster."

"Lobster I know. What exactly are ribs?"

I simply said, "You know? Oink oink. Ribs."

"Oh, those kind of ribs," she said with a new awareness.

"But we often expressed our Jewishness in what we ate," I stated. "We were culinary Jews. We liked chopped liver, gefilte fish, bagels, and of course Reuben sandwiches ... wow, were they good."

"Reuben sandwiches are not kosher," she stated dryly.

"What are you talking about? Reuben sandwiches are of course kosher. They're like ... They're like ..." I searched for an appropriate comparison. "They are the Yom Kippur of the Jewish gastronomical world."

"Well, let's see," she held out her two open palms. "Two pieces of rye bread. On the one we have succulent sliced corned beef. And on the other we have thick slabs of creamy Swiss cheese. Add sauerkraut and slap on some Russian dressing ... we put our two hands together." She clapped her hands together loudly, "... and we get a Reuben sandwich. What do you think? Kosher or not kosher?"

Of course. Milk and meat. A big no, no.

"*Treif.* Definitely not kosher."

"I rest my case," she said flipping her hands upwards in victory.

"So, you see that my family was technically Jewish but definitely not religious. That is, we did not follow any religion. We took the good things from all of them. We celebrated Christmas and Chanukah, Passover and Easter. Why not? It was only after I was shot that I began to look for a little meaning in my life. For the first two years I took lessons at the *Yeshiva* and then eight months ago I put on this funny outfit and started studying in earnest."

"Have you found what you were looking for?" she asked with concern.

Another question from left field. She doesn't pull any punches.

"No, I haven't. Not completely," I said in all honesty. "But for the first time I feel that I really have my feet on the ground. And this stability gives me a perspective I never had before. Most of all, it feels good."

"The suit makes you feel good?"

"It has nothing to do with the suit. It's the belief in God, in his Torah, in keeping the *mitzvos* – commandments- , in keeping the Sabbath, eating kosher. It all feels good. Like my body and my soul can thrive in such an environment. I can see the world now like I never saw it before."

I stopped speaking and pick up the rifle. I fired off my remaining fifteen imaginary bullets and sent the bears howling.

I am a menace with an electronic rifle.

All the while Dafna had been silent, but I could feel that she had been staring at me. When I put the rifle back in its stand she said, "Mr. Lincoln, you impress the heck out of me. I had no idea you were such a philosopher."

"Well, you asked," I said in my defense.

"And you, surely answered," she said with a nod. "And now it is time for air hockey. You may be better than me with the rifle but I am going to beat the pants off you in air hockey."

She did not beat the pants off me, but she was darn good. She was quicker than me but I had a longer reach. We played half a dozen games and split fifty fifty. Our appointment with the *rebbitzen* was in fifteen minutes so we just called our air hockey showdown a draw.

We exited Pinball Pete's and were going down the alley to the car. Coming towards us was a young man in an oversized military style camouflage jacket, dirty black cargo pants and scuffed gym shoes. He was bare headed and his hair was matted, like it had not been washed in quite a while. When we got close, the young man turned and pulled up his jacket pocket and aimed it at us, "I've got a gun. Give me your money."

By instinct I stepped in front of Dafna and said calmly, "Okay, just take it easy. I'll give you want you want."

"Smart thinking," said the young man nervously.

The guy could have been anywhere from fifteen to thirty. I guessed he was younger and that the tough street life was aging him fast ... in more ways than one. I could see the telltale signs of withdrawal — tremor in the hands, erratic movement and speech. This kid was going to do whatever it took to get enough money to make a score of whatever substance it was that was killing him slowly. I was not sure he actually had a gun in his pocket, but I was not going to take the chance. I knew from personal experience that anyone could act the hero, but heroes could also get shot. Besides, I did not have my weapon with me. The kid was obviously an amateur. No professional would stand so close or keep his piece in his pocket. I could easily disable him, but there was a real possibility that he did have gun in his pocket and I was worried about Dafna.

Best to just give him the money.

I was trying to pull my wallet out of my pocket when Dafna stepped around me and said, "You're not really going to give this guy your money, are you?"

"Well, actually, yes I am," I said honestly.

"Shut up lady," said the kid.

Dafna turned to the guy and said threateningly, "You don't know who you are dealing with."

"I'm dealing with a rich guy who is going to give me his money."

"This punk doesn't even have gun," taunted Dafna. "That's probably just his finger in his pocket."

Why was she going out of her way to tick this guy off?

The young man then pulled out a Saturday night special, which was just a little bigger than his palm, and aimed it at Dafna, "You mean like this little 38 Caliber Finger?"

"How do you know we don't also have a gun?" she said defiantly.

"Some people might carry guns, but Jew boys like him don't," said the kid with conviction. "Give me the money, I haven't got all day."

Amazing. This punk was able to recognize a *yeshiva bocher*. He must not be from around here. Very likely a former student at MSU. Interesting.

"You know the police station is just around the corner," Dafna warned our robber. "They're going to catch you."

I could see that she was not going to stop pestering the already jittery addict and this could get dangerous. The kid was already in the shakes and most likely was not going to act rationally. I turned to Dafna and said, "Would you just shut up. You're going to make this young man nervous and we want him to remain calm."

"That's it? This is what a big tough cop and hardnosed investigator does? Some punk waves a gun and you knuckle under? Pull out your gun and shoot the guy," she demanded.

I turned to Dafna and said slowly, "I do not have my pistol with me. Let us just give the man what he wants and have him go away."

"You didn't bring your gun?" she asked incredulously. "How can you investigate a case without a weapon?"

"This was supposed to be a routine simple investigation," I said in my defense. "I did not think bringing my pistol was necessary. So, the best thing to do is give the fellow our money ... nice and easy ... and let the police handle it from here."

"No way! This is my case. My case," she repeated in anger. "I did not take four years of *Krav Magah* lessons at the Detroit Jewish Center to allow some punk to walk all over me."

"Dafna," I said loudly. "This is not part of the case and you have two daughters to think about."

"I am thinking about them. I don't want them to think that I am some wimp who lets a street punk get the better of me. Not like some investigators I know."

The young hoodlum was dumbfounded by our exchange, and that was probably the reason that he did not notice when Dafna sank lower on her left leg and pulled her right leg way back. Then, with an amazing amount of speed and energy she swung her right foot directly into his groin and tender parts.

You could see the pain shoot up from his crotch to the top of his head. His eyes opened wide and his mouth dropped open in surprise. His eyeballs then rolled upwards.

The fellow did not make a sound, but that was understandable since he was not breathing.

Whoa ... that gotta hurt.

Apparently the kick also put Dafna in some pain because she was hopping on her left foot and howling.

The punk grabbed himself between the legs.

I suppose he was wondering if any of his personal paraphernalia was still intact and whether it would be available for future use.

I took the opportunity to remove the gun from the young gentleman's hand and at the same time I held him against the wall. He still had not commenced breathing and if I was not holding him up he would be on the floor in a crumpled mass. This guy was not going anywhere on his own steam. I told him, "Try to take a breath."

Still not breathing but he was getting ready to do so.

I pulled out my phone and called the police emergency number.

Dafna was trying to walk around without wincing in pain. She had soft shoes and she might have broken a toe, "Next time you kick someone in the nads wear a thick sole shoe. Army boots are best."

"Now you tell me," she said in obvious pain.

The police arrived in under five minutes.

Not a great response time considering the station was only about three hundred yards away.

The police asked the usual preliminary questions and took the young perpetrator and his gun into custody. He was still clutching himself and moaning loudly and the police decided they wanted to get him over to the emergency room pronto. They just wrote down our names and contact numbers and told Dafna and me that we could give our statements the next morning before we met with detective Dalton.

We were now about one half hour late for our appointment with the *Rebbitzen* and went to Dafna's car — "I think I better drive. You should rest your foot."

She did not protest and threw me her keys. I pressed the alarm and the car chirped alive. Dafna got in the passenger side and I tried to squeeze into the driver's seat.

No chance.

I was about ten inches taller than Dafna and about one hundred pounds heavier. There just was not enough room for me between the steering wheel and the seat back. I took a moment to move the seat all the way back and then lower it completely. Then I adjusted the mirrors so I could see around the car. I hit the ignition and the car started right up. I shifted to 'drive' and was about to press on the gas pedal when I realized that Dafna had not been speaking these last few minutes. Highly unusual. Up to now she had been a chatterbox.

I put the car back into 'park'.

I looked at Dafna.   Her eyes were glazed and she was staring straight ahead out through the windshield.

Uh oh.

Over the years I had seen this type of reaction.   It happens in victims and their families just after the danger has passed. Somehow people can do some pretty amazing — and sometimes stupid — things in times of stress. They are able to overcome fears and dangers that normally would incapacitate them. The police docs said it comes from an adrenaline rush in times of danger. Problem is that once the adrenaline wears off, the victims suddenly realize the gravity of the actual danger they had been in. For some people the reliving of the event could become overwhelming.   Some even crash.   I even remember one case where the victim had recurrent fears and nightmares and had to be hospitalized for an extended period.

Dafna had that look.

"Dafna," I said softly. "Can you hear me?"

No response.

Not good.

The police shrinks told us to reassure the victims in times like these. Let them know they are safe. Even lie to them and belittle the danger they had been in.

"Dafna," I tried again. "You know I had it covered. There was no way I was going to let that little punk hurt you. You did good. Everything is fine now. You are safe. I am here for you."

Still no reaction.

I tried once more, "Can you hear me?"

She suddenly broke from her reverie and turned slowly in my direction, as if she just noticed that I was in the car. Her next few words were critical in determining her future mental health.

I was worried.

She began nodding her head as a smile broke out on her face, "What a feeling. What a rush. I kicked some serious *tuchis* just now. Nobody messes around with Dafna Lachler when she is on a case," she said proudly.

What was she talking about? "I told you, the attempted robbery had nothing to do with the case?"

"I know that." She paused to point her index finger at me, "But when Dafna Lachler is on the job ... Dafna Lachler is on the job."

I had no idea what that meant and I was not going to ask.

I put the car in drive and started out of the lot, "We're late. Give me directions to *Rebbitzen* Klein's house."

"Make a right," she commanded loudly. "We're on our way to *Rebbitzen* Klein's house and we are going to kick some more *tuchis*."

The woman is totally nuts.

CHAPTER EIGHT — *Meeting Cancelled*

WHEN WE PULLED UP in front of the Klein residence Dafna said, "Just like I figured, she's not home."

"Who's not home?" I asked.

"Devorah Klein."

"How do you know? We haven't even knocked on the door."

"She has a Volvo station wagon. She never goes anywhere without it. She'll even take it to go around the block. It's not in the driveway, so that means she's out," she said with certainty. "Wait here, I'll check the door."

"How could she be out? You made an appointment. I heard her say she'll be happy to see you," I stated.

"That's just Devorah Klein at her best. You're late by two or three minutes. Meeting cancelled. Wait here a moment."

Dafna opened the door and heaved herself up on her bad foot. She limped up the front path, took something off the screen door, then limped back to the car and climbed in. In her hand was a note, "It says, 'Dafnaleh' ...". — She put the letter aside and said, "Many people call me 'Dafnaleh'."

"That's a nice name. I'll remember that," I said jokingly.

She looked at me menacingly, "I hate it. You call me 'Dafnaleh' you get zip from the disks. Is that understood?"

"It sure is Dafna l ... l ...". — I stretched out the 'l' sound, and then added, "Lachler."

"Very funny. The rest of the note says, 'You are late. Out running errands. Back in 45'. It's signed Devorah."

"Isn't that a little strange?"

"Not for Devorah," She said as she handed me the note. "Look at her penmanship."

I looked at the note and was astounded to see a hand written message in which every line was perfectly straight. I mean perfect. In addition every letter was formed and curled just like on the penmanship placards that used to adorn the walls of my third grade class. "I have never seen anything like this. It is way up on the weird list."

"In case you haven't figured it out yet ... Devorah is a perfectionist."

"Like in OCD?" I asked.

"Just like in OCD," Dafna said with a head nod. "But we all love her so much. She is the backbone of the community. She supports everything that is Jewish in the Greater Lansing area to an unbelievable degree. She's there night and day for anyone that is in need. She was a science teacher before they moved here and since I homeschool my girls, she volunteered to teach them science. Add to that her total devotion to her husband. So, we have learned to live with her ... little traits. She means well."

"So we just wait?" I asked.

"We just wait," she said. "You can bet that she will be back exactly forty five minutes from when she wrote the note, but we don't know when that was. We were busy kicking *tuchis*."

"We ... were not kicking *tuchis* ... you ... were kicking *tuchis*. I was an innocent bystander."

"You are darn right," she said with an ecstatic smile. "It was me! I have never felt so alive. I was born for this."

"Whoa, slow down," I said holding up a palm like a traffic cop. "If you get such a high from kicking a guy in the testicles I can hardly wait to see what you will be like when you shoot someone."

"Really, really," she exclaimed with eagerness. "You're going to let me shoot someone? Wow!!! Great!!!"

What kind of a monster have I created here?

"I was kidding," I said in earnest. "You are not getting anywhere near a gun."

"I know," she said with a coy smile. "I just enjoyed yanking your chain."

Dafna could also be a little strange. Had to keep that in mind.

Something she had said earlier bothered me and I wanted her to clarify it for me. "You told me before that you had a score to settle with God because your husband passed away."

"That's right I do. What about it?" she asked.

"Now don't get me wrong. I'm not being judgmental. I just do not understand."

"What is it you do not understand?"

"I have almost a zero knowledge of Jewish philosophy," I said trying to let her know my limitations. "But from what I have been told up til now, *frum* people are expected to simply accept the decisions made by God. You are not supposed to complain about how the Almighty took your husband before his time and left you to take care of the family on your own. So, why is it that you have a score to settle with God."

"You think the score I have to settle with God is based on my suffering? Because I got a raw deal I have bitterness towards God? Is that what you think?"

"Yeah, sure. Isn't it obvious?" I stated.

"No, it's not obvious, because that is not the score I have to settle."

"I'm lost here," I said in a quandary.

Dafna did not say anything at first. She seemed to make a mental decision and began to speak slowly, "David being taken from us so early is part of the Almighty's heavenly plan and I will never know what he was thinking. That's God's way and I accept it. The fact that I have to work harder for my business for my girls ... I accept that too. What I cannot accept is why my David, my *tzadik* of a husband, had to suffer so much for over a year. Three surgeries, chemotherapy, radiation therapy ... he never complained. Not once. He would not take his pain medicines because it clouded his mind and he could not learn the Torah that he loved so much. He could barely walk but he insisted that I take him to the *kollel* twice a day so that they would not have a problem in making the *minyan*. No one saw how much he sacrificed. My question to God is, why David? I said he was a *tzadik* — a holy person. He had only pure wonderful thoughts. All the years I was with him he strove to rid himself of the harmful internal and external influences that make people do bad things. He was above that ... but he was still a real *mensch*. A down to earth real person. He loved me and the girls with all his heart. Why did he have to endure such pain? Why didn't God give some of the pain and suffering to me? I was more than willing to take on the pain, just so that David could be spared even a little of what he went through. He never complained but I could see it in his eyes, he suffered so. The Hebrew word for spouse is *ben zoog*. It means one of a pair. David and I were a pair. We were partners. We were supposed to take on the difficulties of this life together. Share in the profits and pay off the debts. But in the end he had to pay all the bad debts on his own. It tore me apart. Just thinking about it right now tears me apart. That's the score I have to settle with God."

She was holding back tears.

My God, what could I say.

"Do you ever have your teeth cleaned?" I ventured.

"What does that have to do with anything?"

"You know, go to the dental hygienist?"

"Sure, I go twice a year," she said with a shrug.

"Is she gentle?"

"You mean ... does it hurt?" she asked.

"Yeah, does it hurt?"

"No it doesn't ... well, most of the time it's fine. No pain."

"My hygienist, Martha, is as gentle as Attila the Hun," I stated succinctly. "When she is done with me the little napkin thingee on my chest is full of blood and the tears are streaming down my cheeks. I scream, howl, squirm, kick, and grab at her hands the entire half hour I am in her chair."

"Sounds terrible. Why do you go to her?"

"Martha has been my dentist's hygienist for years and I'm used to her. It could also be that I am a closet masochist and don't know it."

"Why are you telling me this?"

"Why do I scream and yell when she is torturing me?"

"Obviously, because it hurts."

"That's it exactly. So why didn't David yell and scream when things were hurting him?" I asked rhetorically. "I scream and yell in front of Martha because I couldn't care less about her. It hurts ... I yell. But it sounds to me that you and your husband had a relationship that I never had with my ex. I bet that in your time together whenever you were able to make him happy it made you feel good. And I'm sure he felt the same way."

She closed her eyes and said, "Absolutely."

"And if he was hurting it hurt you as well."

"Oh, so true," she said in a whisper.

"Don't you see," I said. "You were there with him throughout the ordeal."

"Every day," she said swallowing hard.

"David knew that every show of pain ... every wince ... no matter how small ... would be noticed by you. And when you noticed it caused you pain. And that hurt him even more. He could not be the source of your pain. It probably tore him apart worse than the cancer that was killing him. Every time he faked it ... put on a smile instead of a frown ... he was actually showing his love for you. Your just being there with him showed your love in return. Sounds to me that at the last, it was just an overwhelming expression of love. To me it seems beautiful."

Dafna went silent and then the tears started down her cheeks. She swallowed hard and said softly, "I miss him so. I miss him so."

I should have kept my big mouth shut.

What was I doing philosophizing about love and relationships. My love life has always been one disaster after another. Now look at what I have done.

Dafna used a tissue to blot up her tears and said, "I'm sorry. I've never done that before. And certainly not in front of someone I only met a few hours ago."

"But we're partners that kick *Tuchis* together," I said with mock bravado.

She laughed and held a closed fist in the air, "We are that. Dafna Lachler is on the job."

Suddenly there was a loud tapping of metal on glass and I saw a woman leaning over rapping the ring on her finger against the windshield.

The forty five minutes were up and *Rebbitzen* Klein had come home.

She signaled for us to join her.

Dafna sniffed up her tears and signaled with her thumb for us to head up to the house.

Time to kick some more *tuchis*.

CHAPTER NINE — *Good Housekeeping*

IN MY OFFICIAL CAPACITY as a police officer and detective, I had entered thousands of homes and over the years I learned that the vibes you experienced in the first ten seconds after crossing the threshold were indicative of the internal dynamic of the people that lived in any abode. To analyze these vibes required the use of all your five senses plus that sixth sense that law officials develop — or don't develop.

Every home is different and each has its telltale signs. Some have signs left by younger or older children. Some people are overly messy or overly neat. Some consider cleanliness a recommendation but not a requirement. In some homes there are couples, in others singles. Old. Young. Aged. Neurotic. Pets. Smells. Cooking. Hobbies. Obsessions.

There were signs if you knew what to look for.

They came in all shapes and sizes.

The Klein household was weird.

I was not sure what it was but I was getting a sensation that something was off.

I tried to figure it out.

The first thing I noticed was that the place was immaculate. I was sure that if I ran a hand over the top edge of any of the picture frames I would not find a speck of dust. Every leaf on every plant in the house was shiny clean.

That kind of immaculate.

The rays of light from the late afternoon sun made rainbow hues as they glistened through the polished crystal pendants of the glass chandelier in the formal dining room. The wooden floors of the hallway and living room shone brightly. All the furniture sparkled. The art work on the walls was subdued and appropriate. Small cutesy knickknacks and souvenirs of past vacations were scattered about the room. There were small potpourri jars at strategic points and their woodsy aroma complimented the baking smells emanating from the kitchen. Even the rabbi's study was a sight to see. Where Rabbi Kalmonowitz's office was a hodgepodge of stacked dusty books, Rabbi Klein's bookcases were orderly and pristine. Every shelf dusted and all the books were lined up in straight neat rows.

Everything about the house said — 'In the category of Best Homemaker, *Rebbitzen* Klein takes first prize'. So what was making me feel odd about the home?

What was it?

The *rebbitzen* invited us into the kitchen and set the kettle to boil on the stove. She seated us along the side of a large wooden table as she busied herself with preparing the tea she had offered.

Dafna and I waited in silence.

I knew from the case record that *Rebbitzen* Klein, maiden name Gorelick, was forty three years old and originally came from New York City. She had been married to the late Rabbi Avraham Klein for almost twenty years. I estimated her height to be around five foot four inches and she was as thin as a rail. Not anorexic thin, but not far off. Her face was elongated and the tip of her beakish nose pulled down every time she made one of her pinched smiles ... which was often. She had almost no breast or butt protuberances to speak of. Being a recent widow, she was, of course, dressed in a shapeless black dress that came down well below her knees. Covering her hair was an exceptionally unstylish shoulder length dark brown wig.

Rebbitzen Klein spoke from the kitchen counter, "So, Dafnaleh, what is wrong with your foot. I saw you limping?"

I've got to give Dafna credit. She did not cringe with the use of the nickname she hated. She just waved her hand deprecatingly and said, "It's nothing. Just bumped my foot against something."

Yeah, like that punk's groin.

I reflected on what she had done and realized that had taken quite a bit of courage ... it was stupid ... but it still took courage. Way to go ... Dafna.

The *rebbitzen* pointed her chin in my direction and asked, "And who is this young *bocher*?"

Young? She was only six years older than me, but I guess when you wear the *bocher* outfit ... you are a *bocher*. Age doesn't matter.

"This is Simon Lincoln, he is learning in the *bais medrash* in Detroit. Before that he made his living as a private investigator," said Dafna.

"How interesting," said the *rebbitzen* blandly.

"*Rav* Kalmonowitz has expressed his concerns regarding the tragic death of *Rav* Avraham, *alav hashalom* — may peace be with him," said Dafna.

During their exchange the *rebbitzen* had brought a tea tray to the table and set a placemat in front of each of us. She moved each placemat back and forth and up and down until it was in the exact correct position she wanted. Then she carefully placed a cup on each saucer, turning them precisely so that the ear of the cup was in proper alignment with the pattern on the plates. She poured tea into each so that the height of the tea was exactly the same in each cup. Finally, she placed the tea on our mats so that each was in an identical position and then pointing to the cruets and canisters on the central tray said, "Help yourself to cream, sugar, lemon, and biscuits."

Obsessive compulsive anyone?

The *rebbitzen* took a chair keeping only half of her behind on the seat, "It warms my heart to know that everyone is still thinking about my husband, *alav hashalom*."

"Anyway," continued Dafna. "Rav Kalmonowitz cannot believe that such a fine rabbi as Rav Avraham took his own life."

"I know, I know," said the *rebbitzen* nodding her head. "It is so hard to believe. But the police ... They say ..."

"Rav Kalmonowitz thinks that maybe the police missed something ... " said Dafna.

The *rebbitzen* stopped nodding her head and looked up in surprise, "*Rebbi* thinks it was not suicide? That someone ...?"

She left the statement unfinished.

"Exactly," said Dafna. "That is where Simon comes in. *Rebbi* has asked that he look into the case to see if he could find something that the police have overlooked."

Rebbitzen Klein swung her eyes in my direction and looked at me intently, "Oh, really. That would be amazing. If you could, it would make such a difference."

There was a flutter in her eyes. My gut was telling me something. Maybe it was not all that amazing. What was that all about?

Perhaps she thought that I would definitely be able to prove that the rabbi's death was not suicide. I did not want her to get her hopes up and said, "I'm just looking at the case and all the material the police collected. I know how difficult unexpected suicides can be for the family and I am not sure I will find anything that will change the verdict in the cause of death."

"No matter what, your efforts will be highly appreciated," said the *rebbitzen* earnestly.

"Simon is a terrific investigator," said Dafna encouragingly.

"I am so glad to hear that," said *Rebbitzen* Klein.

"And I am going to assist him in the investigation," stated Dafna proudly.

"Well, good for you," said the *rebbitzen* with enthusiasm.

There was that little eye flutter again.

I decided to start off with the private psychiatric clinic brochures and I asked, "Did you know that Rabbi Klein had a file filled with brochures from psychiatric clinics in his desk?"

"Of course I knew," she answered disdainfully. As if saying 'How could there be anything in this house that I do not know about?'.

"Did he have a problem that needed treatment?"

The *rebbitzen* did not respond immediately and was framing her response. "He told me that he was going to take a break. A break from his teaching and his counseling. He had given it much thought. A break that required more than just going on holiday for a break. He was such a good man. *Mamash a'tzadik.*" I knew that meant he was a saint. She continued, "But he was tired. Impatient. We decided to look into appropriate private clinics. I knew that our community would not be overly understanding if a person required psychiatric treatment. It would tarnish their name forever."

"How did he get this material? E-mail? Fax? Phone call?" I inquired.

"We both went to look at the various clinics personally. We were looking for the most suitable place," she said pinching her little mouth together and nodding her head. "Every time we kept saying that it was not the right place. Oy, how I wish I had been more insistent. Maybe if treatment had been started earlier he would be alive today. I feel so responsible," she said tearfully.

"Devorah, Devorah," said Dafna. "You did everything you could. The whole community saw how you always supported *Reb* Avraham. Your relationship was envied by all of us. You were our example of what a good marriage should be like. You should not feel responsible. You could not have known."

"Thank you for those kind words," said the *rebbitzen* snuffling up her tears.

We spent the next half hour going over the routine questions concerning an unexpected death. She confirmed just about everything that the police reported. The only new bit of information was that the Rabbi did his counseling for troubled Jewish students at the Hillel House just off the MSU campus. She ran us through what happened on the night she discovered the body and showed us the basement. A spotlessly clean super tidy basement. Someone had even cleaned out every shred of lint from the dryer filter. Now, how strange is that?

OCD rules.

Creepy.

The *rebbitzen* and Dafna went back to sit in the kitchen and I inspected the alarm system very closely looking to find how someone could possibly get into the house without tripping the alarm. I had been hoping to find a bypass switch on the back door. Many homes have them so that the alarm for the rest of the house stays on while the family could come and go through the garden door. I looked everywhere but did not find such a switch nor anything else that was amiss. The only vulnerable spot was the roof space but there was no way that anyone could get in without being noticed by the neighbors.

We left the house with *Rebbitzen* Klein telling us to come back if we had more questions or if we wanted to inspect anything else. She then wished us luck and success in our investigation. Her parting words to Dafna were words of caution, "Dafnaleh, be careful. If Avraham did not take his own life there could be dangerous people out there. I don't want anything to happen to you."

Did she know something she was not telling us?

We climbed into Dafna's car and when I turned to her I said jokingly, "If I had to live with that woman in that house, I think I would also take my own life."

"Don't even joke about that," she scolded me. "They were the most devoted couple I have ever seen. And what's wrong with her house?"

"Are you kidding me," I asked. "It's like a museum or an art exhibit or a showplace ... I don't know how to classify it. People don't live in such houses."

"Yes, Devorah can be a little intense when it comes to housekeeping."

Then it dawned on me.

I knew what was bothering me about the house.

Her entire house looked like it was being prepared for a photo shoot for Good Housekeeping. Any moment the photographers were going to set up the tripods and lights. It all had to be perfect. The façade had to be perfect. But it was still a façade. The Klein house was not a place in which people lived. I did not know what it was that the Kleins did in that house or what kind of a relationship they had, but they did not live there.

I was not ready to share these thoughts with Dafna and said, "Let's get back to your house so I can pick up my car. It's getting late and I want to make it back to the *kollel* for afternoon services."

"Good idea," agreed Dafna. "It is late and I know there are no kosher restaurants in this area. If you like you can have supper with us … we always have plenty."

That was a nice gesture and for some reason I just knew that I would enjoy a meal with her family. Still, I only just met Dafna a few hours ago and even though we had definitely cemented our partnership by kicking *tuchis* together, it was too much too soon. I might be reading too much into the invitation. I need to put any such thoughts on hold until the case is over. "Thank you, but no thanks," I replied. "I stocked up before I came. I've got a bunch of scrumptious takeaway meals from One Stop at the motel."

"Oh, please. I'm sure the girls would love to talk to you some more and I guarantee whatever my mother has cooked is better than whatever you have waiting for you. Besides I could use the time to look through the case material before we see Detective Dalton in the morning."

"No can do, I told you, I have a rule that no one sees any of my evidence before I do. And my first look through is slow and thorough. I need the time. I'll let you see the stuff tomorrow."

"So what am I supposed to do for now?" she asked.

"Go home and kick some *tuchis* with those disks."

CHAPTER TEN— *Semper Fidelis*

AFTERNOON PRAYERS WERE HELD just as the sun began to set and they were followed by evening prayers. In between, there was a twenty minute lesson delivered by Rabbi Lipsky. It was not the most inspiring talk I had ever heard, but it was not bad for a rabbi that normally did not teach. Altogether we were eleven men at services and I could see three of the men eyeing me. These were the volunteers who came to fill the required ten count for the *minyan*. I suppose each was thinking that if I was going to be at the *minyan* anyway, Rabbi Lipsky should have kept them informed so that one of the volunteers could have stayed home.

As I drove back to the hotel, I thought about what Dafna had asked me about my discharge from the Marines.

I usually try not to think about it.

I was twenty years old and had been in the Marines for almost two years. I really liked it. For most of my time, I had been assigned to the 1st Battalion of 1st Marine Regiment of the 1st Marine Division stationed in Fort Pendleton, California. I felt like it was my home and was seriously considering re-upping as a first step in a glorious military career.

I was young. I was stupid.

One day, out of the blue, I was ordered to report to a Captain Flowers' office. I do not remember what his official capacity was on the base, but he was not in my chain of command so the order was a little out of the ordinary. But when you are a Marine and an officer, any officer, tells you to jump, all you can say is, 'How high?'.

The muscular captain was two inches taller than me and about eighty pounds heavier. His short blond hair was cut in the white sidewall style and if you ran your finger over the crease in his pants you would come away with a bleeding laceration.

That kind of Marine.

The captain told me that he was arranging a demonstration of hand to hand combat for the base I had been 'volunteered' to participate. He informed me of the place and time and ordered me to be there.

I had no idea what the captain was talking about so I asked my platoon sergeant. His first words were, "Oh, crap. He is doing that s**t again. I thought he stopped."

It turns out that Captain Flowers was a devout believer in White Aryan Supremacy and preached its dogma to any that would listen. In the past, to prove the inferiority of non-Aryans, he would stage hand to hand combat demonstrations and as 'luck' would have it, the person who 'volunteered' to be his sparring partner was always either black, Hispanic or Jewish. Captain Flowers had been a Marine champion in hand to hand combat and when the demonstrations were over the volunteer usually required hospitalization. His superiors reprimanded him for his behavior and the demonstrations had stopped. No real punishment was ever meted out because no Marine regulations were actually violated. Captain Flowers was always very careful in how he worded everything he did. But his climb up the promotion ladder came to a halt. His rank did not change and he would still be a captain when he retired next year.

"That son of a bitch wants to get another notch on his belt before he retires," said my sergeant. "You ain't black and you ain't a Chicano. Why did he choose you?"

When I told my sergeant that I was Jewish he was absolutely floored because I had never, ever, mentioned my ethnic background.

My sergeant told me, "Flowers especially hates Jews and you being tall, blue-eyed and blonde probably pisses him off something fierce."

A Jew had no right looking like an Aryan.

He then explained the precarious situation that I was in. The options he outlined went from bad to worse: If I went to my superiors and filed a complaint of anti-Semitism against Captain Flowers, it would be dismissed because there was no evidence that the captain had done anything to me that had an anti-Semitic basis. If I went to my own regimental command and asked that they intervene and get me out of the demonstration, then I would be considered a big baby running home to mama. It would look bad on my record. If I did not show up for the demonstration, the captain could file charges against me for not obeying an officer. His recommendation was for me to show up, get the s**t beaten out of me, and keep my mouth shut. He assured me that if the beating was getting too intense, someone would intervene.

Getting the living daylights knocked out of me would accomplish a number of things. Flowers would get to show the world that Jews cannot stand up against the white Aryan race and what a big man he is. The senior officers and the Marine Corps would once again be relieved of having to officially deal with Captain Flowers and his racial bias. While at the same time everyone would know that I took it like a man.

Hopefully.

To me, it seemed that all the options were crappy choices.

The whole situation was seriously bothering me emotionally. It was not the impending beating that disturbed me ... although I anticipated that with trepidation ... it was that this was my very first encounter with real unadulterated anti-Semitism. I knew that anti-Semitism existed and in high school we had learned a little about the Holocaust, but I had never experienced it firsthand. I had been raised in Bloomfield Hills, Michigan. Half of my high school class was white gentile and the other half was a mixture of blacks, Hispanics, Orientals, and Jews. We would constantly make lighthearted fun of our different ethnic backgrounds, but hatred based on someone's race or color was unheard of. My friends came from all ethnic groups and races.

I understood that sometimes people did bad things to one another and hatreds develop. But what I could not fathom was the idea that someone hated someone else not because they had done something but because they simply existed. I barely knew that I was Jewish, but for Flowers my Jewishness meant I did not have the right to exist in his vicinity, in his country or in his world.

I could not believe that this was happening in the Marine Corps that was supposed to be my home.

Unbelievable.

On the day of the demonstration, the sergeants from the other two platoons came to visit me and they both gave me the same advice as my own sergeant. I should allow myself to be the captain's punching bag and keep my mouth shut. And most important … 'Whatever you do … don't fight back', because Flowers would most definitely get angry and he could 'accidentally' deliver a lethal blow by mistake.

I was not filled with optimism.

There was one little bit of information that Captain Flowers and the rest of the Corps did not know.

I had been a terrible student in junior high and high school. Nowadays, I probably would be diagnosed as ADD, or ADHD, or some other behavioral malady with exotic initials. About the only activity I enjoyed and excelled in, was martial arts. My folks shelled out a lot of money to send me to judo, karate, and aikido classes. I was darned good at them all. My senseis all said that I had reached the black belt level in all three. I practiced on my own to stay limber, but I never demonstrated my skills in the Marines because I did not want to draw attention to myself.

So what to do? If I used my training and fought back I might get killed. The captain was bigger and stronger than me. Not a pleasant thought. Or I could be his punching bag and hopefully live to talk about it.

I arrived at the gymnasium and found that there were about two hundred enlisted men and noncoms gathered around the mat. Not an officer in the group. My sergeant told me that all the officers knew about the demonstration and found it advantageous not to be there. I changed into shorts, t-shirt, and gym shoes and waited. Captain Flowers arrived right on time already dressed for the demonstration.

The muscular officer looked both impressive and menacing. If he was trying to scare me he had accomplished his mission.

The captain had everyone move off the mat and then gave a short talk about the importance of developing hand to hand skills as a Marine. We began the demonstration with him asking me to attack him in various ways — with a wooden knife, with a stick, with a garrote — and he would demonstrate the classic ways of combating these attacks.

All straight forward.

Then he said that we would practice freestyle. He was going to let me attack him anyway I liked and he would show the group how he defended himself.

That was the signal for it to begin.

I was going to get the s**t beaten out of me and I did not relish the thought.

I came at the captain in a feeble attack and he threw me to the mat with ease. He asked me to try again and once more I lasted only five seconds.

When he hoisted me to my feet he spoke into my ear so only I could hear, "You little piece of Jewish s**t, I'm going to finish off what Hitler started. You are never going to see you mama again. Kiss your ass goodbye."

He came at me with a frightening intensity. I tried to defend myself but he punched me in the ribs very hard and I heard something break. He then head butted me and only by pure luck my nose was not broken. My head was spinning. He was punching at my face and body mercilessly and was kicking me with his legs at every opportunity. My face would be black and blue for weeks. Then he threw me to the ground, wrapped his right arm around my throat and began choking me. I tried to pull his hand away but Flowers' muscular arm was twice the size of mine and it was useless. He used his free left hand to gouge at my eyes and only by twisting my head about and pushing his hand, did I keep his fingers from injuring my eyes.

I could not breathe, and I knew I could never overcome his superior strength, so I gave him the three quick pats on his shoulder. That was the universal signal used in all combative sports to say 'I give up'.

Flowers did not relent.

This was no longer a demonstration.

Captain Flowers had crossed the line.

His intent was to cause me permanent injury.

I was being strangled to death. I squirmed and tossed my head to prevent Flowers from blinding me.

What the captain was doing had to be obvious to all the spectators and I expected one of them to come forward to stop the match.

Okay, guys ... break up the fight.

The captain had done his thing. I had done mine. Everyone did what they were supposed to do. Let us call this demonstration over so we could get back to our lives.

He continued to choke me.

I was not breathing.

Everything was going grey.

No one came.

I had been willing to be a punching bag ... but I drew the line at being a corpse.

I decided, I would fight back.

There was not much time because I would soon lose consciousness.

I concentrated my ki as my sensei had instructed me.

As Flowers choked me his head was resting just over my left shoulder. It was the only area that was vulnerable. What I was about to do was definitely not in the Kodokan rules of the sport.

I did not have much room to swing my arm. I saw my target as a point about one foot behind the captain's head. With all my ki and all my power I brought my right hand around in a looping blow to the captain's face. I am not sure what I hit, but it was enough force to make him loosen his head hold.

I scrambled free and gasped for air. When I got to my feet I took a loose stance in front of him.

The grey was lifting slowly.

The captain rubbed his forehead and looked at me. He squared off before me, laughed out loud and said to the crowd, "Look at this, would you believe it. Our little Hebrew friend wants to play. So, let's play."

The captain attacked quickly and I sidestepped his grasp. I bobbed and weaved and his punches went wide. He began to get angry.

Angry is good. You get sloppy when you are angry.

Once more he came towards me with great force and I used his momentum to throw him over my hip to the mat. On his next attack he came in low. I avoided his advance and as his body went by I punched him hard in the back of the neck sending him to the floor once more.

He was fuming.

Even better.

He came at me with high roundhouse kicks aimed at my head which I easily avoided. I knew all these preliminary kicks were to keep me off balance so that he could land a more powerful kick with his preferred right leg. He advanced rapidly to get all of his weight behind this blow. He shot his right leg out in my direction.

I had been waiting for this.

I grasped the ankle of his raised leg in my left hand and to supplement his forward motion I spun to my left. This pulled him even more rapidly towards me. I was now facing away from him and I drove the right side of my body into his elevated leg. All the power of his forward inertia, my sideways motion and the leverage I had on his leg were combined to act on his right knee. We both landed on the mat with a loud thud and when I got up Captain Flowers' knee now bent in an entirely new direction. He was screaming on the floor and the medics were summoned.

A sergeant I did not recognize came quickly to my side and hustled me out of the gym. "Let's get you out of here before any of Flowers' White Supremacy buddies get any ideas," he said. "That was beautiful. Very stupid ... but beautiful."

The captain suffered a shattered knee which put an end to his Marine career. At the official inquiry the other officers in his unit said that they were not aware of any hidden agenda associated with the captain's demonstrations. Meaning he was never anti-black, anti-Hispanic or an anti-Semite. Just a good natured salt of the earth Marine captain. It was all a general whitewash of the events so that the captain would not lose his Marine pension.

After the inquiry, the senior officers delivered an unofficial message to the junior officers and they passed it along to the noncoms, who finally passed it to my sergeant, who passed it to me. The message was that I had made the wrong choice. I should not have defended myself ... even if the cost to me would have been severe. I should have taken a beating and just shut up. I should have done it for the Corps. By fighting back and beating the captain an official inquiry had to be conducted. The Corps did not wash its dirty linen in public. I was respectfully asked not to consider staying in the service. They also let me know that if I did not take their suggestion they would be obligated to file charges against me for assaulting a senior officer with intent to cause serious bodily harm.

I got my honorary discharge from the Marines, but there was no honor in it at all.

CHAPTER ELEVEN — Pancakes

I GOT BACK TO the Marriott at about 9:00 PM and nuked two of the dinners in the microwave. How they expected a grown man to live on what was included in a single dinner was beyond me. When they were hot, I placed them side by side on the desk, opened a couple of cans of pop and ripped open a bag of chips.

Nothing like good healthy nutritious food.

The first thing I did was go over my notes of what we had done during the day. Then I reread them and made corrections. The attempted mugging was not included.

As I gulped down my food, I retrieved the case file and began reading.

I kept at it, reading the material again and again for almost two hours. I could almost quote every page.

I put the file aside and took out my laptop and inserted the photographic disk.

Before looking at the pictures, I transferred a copy of all the images to my phone, in case I wanted to study the pictures when I was not near my laptop. I started my media program and as soon as the first pictures of the 'crime scene' came up I realized I had a problem. About half of the pictures were of the corpse. As usual, they were pretty gruesome, but as a policeman I had seen thousands of similar pictures. In addition, I had never met the victim when he was alive.

How would Dafna be able to look at the pictures?

Simple ... I would advise her not to look at them. If she insists, I will try to warn her about what she is going to see. I do not know how she will react. Whatever happens ... happens.

I ran through the pictures a couple dozen times and studied each picture individually. The police had made a video shot from the entrance door to the basement and then made a long single shot walking through the entire house as it appeared that night.

Did I see anything in the pictures that made me suspicious of foul play?

Not a thing.

But there was one thing that was bothering me. It was something that was not in the photos.

The coroner's report said that the corpse was dressed in his pajamas and after death the body lost sphincter control. Meaning he peed and/or pooped. This was confirmed by the soiling of the pajamas. But where was the rest of the pee. The cloth of the pajamas can only absorb a small amount of the urine. Almost always there is a small puddle under the body. None was reported and there was no sign of it in the pictures.

My devious detective's mind is playing games with me.

Because, if it is not suicide, then he must have died somewhere else. But if that was true, how did his body get up into the noose in the basement? He was not a small man. Furthermore, if he died somewhere else in the house, we still had no idea how the puddle of urine had disappeared.

I knew that there were a number of physiological phenomena that could explain the puddle puzzle, but these were rare occurrences. Common things occur commonly, rare things occur rarely.

Still it was strange.

It was close to 2:00 am, when I put the file down and went to sleep.

Morning prayers wait for no one ... unless of course you are the missing tenth man to make the *minyan*.

∞

The alarm sounded at 6:00 am, and I was shaved, showered and dressed by 6:30 am. I took a couple of minutes to fashion three bagel and lox sandwiches, then grabbed my *tallis* and *tefillin* –phylacteries -, my laptop and the case file and I was out the door. Morning prayers at the *kollel* were at 7:00 am, and I did not want to be late.

In the Detroit *bais medrash* the prayers take almost an entire hour. Every separate prayer is recited with extreme devotion. Devotion takes time.

This would not work in the *kollel*.

The three 'volunteers' had to get to work, so, from start to finish was thirty five minutes. Nothing was skipped, but I would not be surprised to learn that the Almighty sometimes had a hard time making out exactly what was said in the Lansing *Kollel*.

I turned down Rabbi Lipsky's offer of a hot breakfast. I showed him my bagel sandwich cache and headed for the *kollel* exit.

I gobbled down the bagels on the way to the Lachler household and punctually, at 8:00 am, I rang Dafna's bell.

I heard a scamper of feet and the front door was swung open by two eager young ladies.

I bowed my head slightly and said in mock seriousness, "Good morning Princess Susie. Good morning Princess Aliza. You both look lovely."

The girls thought this hysterical and burst out laughing. Dafna came to the door and asked, "What's so funny?"

Both girls pointed at me and said in unison, "He is."

Dafna was wearing a baggy long sleeved tan sweater and a black skirt. Didn't she wear anything that was ... feminine? The tent like clothing she seems to prefer could hide the physique of an orangutan. But that was the normal outfit that *frum* ladies wore.

Get used to it.

She looked at her giggling daughters and asked, "What did you say to them?"

With feigned innocence I said, "I just told them how ugly they were and they started laughing. I don't understand it."

"What a liar," screeched Susie.

Aliza followed with a loud, "You did not. You said we looked lovely."

"Me?" I asked. "I said you girls look lovely?"

"Yes, you did," corrected Aliza.

Susie said proudly, "And you called us princesses."

"You ugly girls, princesses? No way," I insisted.

Dafna's daughters broke out in another round of laughter.

"Are you calling my girls ugly?" Dafna scolded playfully.

"Well, maybe they are just a little bit lovely," I said in acquiescence.

"Girls, get back to the table with Bubbi and finish your breakfast," said Dafna.

The girls did not move. They just smiled broadly and looked at me.

Aliza broke the silence with, "Are you going to marry Ima?"

Whoa, where did that come from?

"That's what Bubbi says," added Susie.

Dafna yelled towards the kitchen, "Mom, what are you telling the girls?"

Mrs. Kalin's voice could be heard answering, "Nothing but the truth. And why are you still keeping Mr. Lincoln standing at the door. Invite him in for breakfast."

"I'm sorry," said Dafna apologetically.

"What are you sorry about?" I asked.

"For what my daughters ... and my mother ... ," she did not complete the sentence. "Never mind, please come in. Mom made pancakes in your honor."

Wow, pancakes. I have not had pancakes since I went kosher. My recently consumed triple bagel and lox bagel breakfast had suddenly become a lead weight in my gut, but there was no way I was turning down pancakes.

"Sure, if it's not an imposition. Maybe, just coffee," I said to be polite, but my mind was on pancakes.

She pushed her daughters towards the kitchen, "Get back to the table. Mr. Lincoln is coming in, you won't miss anything." They complied reluctantly. Dafna led the way into the kitchen.

"How's your foot?" I asked.

"Nothing broken, but still a little sore. I'll live."

"Heavy soled shoes ... that's the trick," I advised.

"Believe me, I am going to remember," she said.

The kitchen was filled with breakfast smells. Pancakes on the griddle, orange peels from the freshly squeezed juice, coffee just off the George Clooney machine.

Very homey.

"Have a seat," said Mrs. Kalin. "I'll have pancakes for you in a second."

Just to be polite I said, "Really, there is no need. You don't have to trouble yourself."

Who was I kidding? My mouth was watering just from the smell.

"No bother. If you already dirtied the griddle … you can make one … you can make a dozen. Besides this is the only place in the world you'll get these babies," Dafna's mom said proudly.

"They are known around here as 'blueberry buttermilk pow pancakes'" said Dafna informatively.

The older woman said, "The trick is I heat the buttermilk and melt in three … four tablespoons of grated cheese."

"Mom, they're good, but not that good," said Dafna.

Mrs. Kalin just looked at her daughter and then at me, "You'll see."

Dafna asked, "Did you bring the case file?"

I said, "Of course. It's in the car."

"Well, get it. I have been dying to have a look at it all night," she said.

"You'll have time to read it in the car," I said dismissingly.

"I'll have time to read it right now," she insisted.

"I'm about to have your mother's pancakes. I wouldn't want to offend her. There's no time," I said.

"There's plenty of time," she said in a bossy tone. "Get the case file. You promised."

I looked up at Mrs. Kalin, "Is there time?"

She looked at the griddle and then back at me, "Yeah, there's time."

I did not like Dafna's demanding tone, "You did not say 'please'."

Dafna put a false smile on her face and said, "Please."

It took me about thirty seconds to retrieve the file from the car and return to my seat. I had a stack of four thick pancakes on my plate, a cup of what looked like a cappuccino to its right and a small glass of orange juice to its left.

Dafna grabbed the file out of my hand and pushed away her dishes and cutlery as she began to read.

I said the suitable pre-pancake blessing and cut off a wedge and popped it into my mouth.

Suddenly I had a taste sensation that brought tears to my eyes.

It was so good.

Soft … warm … creamy … sweet … flavorful … fluffy … tart … rich … etc … etc …

Wow, these were good.

Mrs. Kalin was asking me, "So, are they good or what?"

I couldn't speak.

I just wanted more pancakes.

Dafna spoke without raising her head from the page she was reading, "Mom, why did you give him so many. He'll never be able to finish four of those pancakes."

'Bite your tongue. Make me another dozen', I thought to myself.

I was still in a sensory overload and the best I could do was raise my pancake stuffed mouth from my plate and answer Mrs. Kalin's question by putting a beatific smile on my face and nodding my head like an idiot.

Dafna's mom pointed at me and said, "See, he likes them."

Bagels move over. Real food is on the way.

Before I knew what was happening I looked down at my plate and was surprised to see that it was clean.

No trace of the pancakes. Where did they go?

I looked at the kitchen clock and suddenly realized that I had vacuumed up all four of the pancakes in about a minute.

I also realized that to anyone watching me — i.e. the Lachler family — that must have been quite a spectacle. I raised my eyes to see Mrs. Kalin, Susie and Aliza looking at me in silent awe.

Dafna was still flipping pages in the file, but with the silence she looked around inquisitively, "What's going on?"

Aliza broke the silence with, "Boy, you sure eat fast."

I put on a smile and said in my defense, "The pancakes were very good."

"Would you like some more?" asked Mrs. Kalin.

I knew the correct response was to refuse politely. I could not leave these people thinking that I was a pig when it came to food. So I looked up and said, "Yes, Please. I'd love some more."

Mrs. Kalin poured the batter onto the grill and said, "It'll be just a minute."

"Bubbi, I'm done," said Aliza.

Susie followed with, "So, am I."

"Did you say the prayer after eating?" asked Dafna, her head still in the file.

"Yes, Ima," they both said.

Mrs. Kalin added, "You have until 9:00 am, to straighten up your room and then I expect you both in the den for morning lessons."

Susie said, "Yes, Bubbi."

Aliza followed with, "O.K."

Then they both got up and left the room.

"What well behaved children," I commented.

"They sure are," said Mrs. Kalin in agreement.

"Don't be fooled," said Dafna. "Do you know why they are suddenly so well behaved?"

"You mean, they aren't always like this?" I asked.

"Pu-leeeeze," said Dafna. "They are acting like little ladies because my mother told them that if they misbehaved you would not want to marry their Ima."

"Their Ima, being you," I said.

"Exactly."

"Why did you tell him that," asked Mrs. Kalin.

"And why did you tell that to the girls," countered Dafna.

"Desperate times require desperate measures," answered her mother.

"Mom!" said Dafna angrily.

"Here are your pancakes," she said sliding then onto my plate and turning off the griddle. "I'll just go check on the girls. Unless you want some more."

My mouth was already filled with pancake and even though my heart was not in it, I was able to mumble, "No, thanks, this will be fine."

As I ate … more slowly this time … I looked at Dafna. I now noticed that she was almost finished with the entire forty or fifty pages of the file. She seemed to be scanning each page for about five seconds before she moved to the next.

Very sloppy.

The basic tenet of all detective work is studying all the elements and facts in the case slowly and deliberately. Analyzing every word and phrase used by the investigating officers. Because very often some subliminal impression seen by the officer will be transcribed as a cryptic sentence into the written report and it will be the key to solving a case.

Skimming over the case file was a no-no.

She finished the file just as I was finishing my coffee.

George Clooney you make a good cup of java.

Dafna looked up and asked, "Where are the photographs of the crime scene and the corpse?"

"I wanted to talk to you about that," I said hesitatingly. "The pictures are pretty bad and they are of someone you knew. Maybe you shouldn't look at them."

She thought to herself for a moment and said, "You know that I salvage disks for a living." She waited until I nodded in understanding and then continued seriously, "I fix disks that contain information for businesses and private individuals. They need this information or else they would not pay me the big bucks to repair the disks. The thing is, that there is also a lot of personal stuff on these disks. Things the people who own the disks don't want anyone to see. I have to restore it all because I have no idea what the customer absolutely needs and what he absolutely wants buried. I have seen things that go from the ridiculous to pornographic to sadistic to sick and to maybe even criminal. I always say I have seen it all and then along comes the next disk and I realize that I have not. I know seeing Rabbi Klein's corpse will be tough, but I will be looking to help that wonderful man. I was not able to help when he lived. He, or someone else, took his life and I did nothing to prevent that. Maybe I can help him in death."

I pursed my lips together and nodded, "Fine, I have the disk in my laptop. You can see the photos in the car. Let's go."

"Don't forget to say the prayer for after eating pancakes," she said.

I, as yet, did not know all the different prayers by heart. There was a prayer for just about everything you did during the day. I had to rely on the small *siddur* — Jewish prayer book — that I always kept in my inside breast pocket. I took out the *siddur* and looked at Dafna, "Yes, Ima."

CHAPTER TWELVE — *Negel Vasser*

I SAW DAFNA COME OUT of the house carrying a wicker picnic hamper. I asked, "What's that for?"

"My mother figures the best way to a man's heart is through his stomach. Mom made us lunch," she said with a laugh.

If her mother's lunch was as good as her breakfast ... way to go Mrs. Kalin!

Dafna threw the hamper into the back seat and climbed into the car. Her next words were, "Where's your laptop. I want to see the disk."

The computer was in the space between the bucket seats and I handed it to her. I was about to explain the intricacies of my particular laptop but I saw that it would be superfluous. Dafna knew her way around computers.

She was flipping through images before we made the first turn.

Once again she was giving the images only a superficial study. Not good. She needs to get the ground rules of investigating straight in her mind. "Dafna, ... " I began.

"Not now," she snapped back. "I want to see the video before we get to the station."

The police was our first scheduled stop and that was about three minutes away. She had to look at over seven hundred photos and the video ran for seven minutes. No way could she see so much material. I glimpsed in her direction and saw the images flash on the screen for a fraction of a second before the next shot came up.

Very bad.

As I parked the car in front of the station I saw she was watching the video. Somehow she had gotten the video player to go at a really fast speed.

Sloppy, sloppy, sloppy.

"Dafna, we're here. ..." I began.

"Just one second," she said holding up her index finger with eyes glued to the screen. The video ended, she closed the laptop and said, "Now we can go in."

"I wanted to say that reading the file and looking at the images like you did is sloppy detective work," I scolded.

"Don't blame me," she countered. "You only showed me the stuff this morning. I will look at it again."

"And again, and again, and again. Slowly ... meticulously. That's how you solve cases. Skimming leads to mistakes," I warned.

"Who skimmed?" she asked.

"You did. I saw the way you skimmed the case file this morning at breakfast."

"No, that's just the way I read," she explained.

"Nobody reads like that. That's skimming."

"No, really. I do. I read like that," she insisted. "Well actually, you're right. I am not reading. One of the neurophysiologists that studied me said that I don't actually read."

"You were studied by a neurophysio ... whatever?"

"Yeah, about four years ago. One of the professors at the university wanted to know how I process written words so fast. He said I don't read. What I do is absorb an image of the words and then my brain processes the images. I don't read at all. It's all image processing."

"If you don't read, how much time does it take for your brain to do this image processing?" I inquired.

"Oh it's instantaneous," she stated simply. "Same for actual images. It's hard to explain but that's the reason I can find things on disks that other people cannot. I am not looking for information, I am looking for the digital image the information created on the disk. Like recognizing a face in the crowd. Do you understand?"

"Not a word," I said dumbfounded.

"If we have some free time when we are not hunting down nefarious criminals I will try to explain it more clearly."

"Do you remember any of the stuff you see from the images?" I asked.

"All of it," she said. "The professor said I have a true photographic memory."

"And I am supposed to believe that in the last twenty minutes you absorbed and remembered all the material in the files and photographs?"

"Try me," she challenged.

OK, she asked for it.

Game is on.

Last night I studied that file backwards and forwards for over five hours. It was only late in the night that I discovered the puddle puzzle. No way could she have noticed the problem. It required careful scrutiny of the file comparing the notes of the investigating officer, detectives and the CSI. Then it had to be checked with the photographs and coroner's reports. She could not have processed so much material in so short a period of time. And even if she did, she does not have the investigatory experience.

Time to show off.

"Did you notice anything unusual in the case file that might indicate that this was not a suicide?" I said with a smirk.

"Actually, yes," she said. "Why wasn't there any pee on the floor under the body? After all if he was ...."

"Yeah, yeah, very good. You caught that, not bad," I said dismissingly.

Holy cow! She picked up on that. The lady does have a photographic memory. I am thoroughly impressed.

"Also, one more thing" she continued. "If he was planning to kill himself why did he put *Negel Vasser* under his bed? After all, he was not going to use it."

That hit me like a bomb.

The *Negel Vasser*.

How could I be so stupid as to miss that?

Negel Vasser is a custom practiced by very Orthodox Jews. The words in Yiddish literally mean 'water for the nails' and refers to a jug of water and a basin set right next to the bed so that on rising in the morning a person could ritually cleanse his hands before touching anything else.

The photographs and video clearly showed the jug and basin at the bedside and I had identified it for what it was.

Negel Vasser.

The investigating police just wrote it up as a jug of water and the CSI noted that the only prints were those of the victim.

Dafna was absolutely correct. If he was not going to be using the *Negel Vasser* in the morning, why had he put it out?

I missed it completely.

What an idiot I was.

But I was not about to let her know that.

Macho rules. Who is the boss?

As we opened the car doors and climbed out, she said apologetically, "It could be I missed something else. I'll have another look at the material. I am sorry, I don't have your experience."

"Don't feel bad. You're new at this. You cannot be expected to hit a home run the first time at bat," I said trying to hide my embarrassment. "But, keep up the good work. Let's get into the station."

∞

We spent the next forty five minutes giving our statements to a uniformed female police officer. She scrutinized the incident sheet of the attempted robbery outside Pinball Pete's and told us that the kid was now hospitalized in the urology department at the university hospital for 'blunt trauma to the testicles'. He was also in full blown withdrawal and was getting treated for that as well. The punk had made a big mistake by using a gun in an attempted robbery because Michigan has a compulsory three year tag on sentence for anyone using a firearm in a crime. He was going to do hard time.

The officer finished typing into the computer and ran off a hard copy which she stapled to the incident report. "We're done," she said dismissing us. Then she looked at Dafna and asked with concern, "How's your foot?"

"Still a little sore."

"Next time, thick soled shoes. That's the trick," she said with a wink.

∞

We went up to the detectives division to find Julie Dalton. She was waiting for us and we all went to an unoccupied interrogation room to go over the case. Most things were crystal clear and the few that were not, she explained fully.

Living proof of cooperation up the whazoo.

It took an hour and when we were done I had a half page of notes and some ideas of how to proceed with the investigation.

At Dafna's prompting, I mentioned to Dalton the two unusual findings from the case file. That there was no water under the body where it should have been and that there was water in the jug where it should not have been.

It took a while for her to grasp what '*Negel Vasser*' was all about, but she pointed out that these discrepancies did not prove in any way that this was not a suicide. She explained away our findings by saying, "Sometimes there ain't a whole lot of urine. Like maybe he peed before killing himself. And that means no puddle. Also, maybe he decided to kill himself after he put out his 'Neegal Viser'. Show me a motive or a suspect and we'll check further. Until then we are still calling this a suicide."

CHAPTER THIRTEEN — Kaboom

OUR NEXT STOP WAS 'Serenity Spa' on the outskirts of East Lansing. It was a very ... very ... upscale private psychiatric clinic. Obviously it had once been someone's private estate and the main house had been converted into the treatment facility. The caretaker's cottage had been refurbished as the executive offices of the complex and this is where we met with the marketing director/public relations officer/spokesperson of the clinic, Mrs. Catherine Paisley. The sixtyish skinny lady was dressed in a tan blouse with a ruffled V-neck collar over brown tailored pants. Her grey blonde hair was in a neat bun at the back of her head and her glasses were suspended over her scrawny bosom by a braided cord looped around her neck.

"Thank you for seeing us Mrs. Paisley," I said in greeting.

"Please, call me Cathy," she chimed, in an aristocratic Southern drawl.

She had a broad smile across her face but I could tell that it was as real as a three dollar bill. What the ole boys call a 'shit-kickin' grin'. Like she knew something that you did not.

I instinctively felt that this woman did not like me, but as yet could not fathom her reason for doing so. Normally people did not start disliking me until they knew me for a couple of hours.

"Why, thank you, Cathy," I said with an equally false smile.

I noticed that I had reacted to her 'bad' vibes and my tone had become just a little bit condescending. I made an effort to sound more sincere.

"How can I help you," she said, her voice dripping molasses.

She wanted to help me about as much as she wanted a mule to kick her in the head. What a fake.

But, why? Why was she behaving so?

Showing her my ID, I said, "My name is Simon Lincoln and I'm a private investigator. This is my assistant, Dafna Lachler." Cathy seemed surprised, but kept her vapid smile in place. "We are working with the East Lansing police and looking into the death of Rabbi Avraham Klein. We understand that he and his wife were here inquiring about hospitalization. Do you remember them?"

"Of course I do," she said. "Lovely couple."

Liar, liar, pants on fire. She obviously did not think they were a lovely couple.

"Can you tell me anything about the indication for hospitalization here?"

"If you mean why here, then the answer is because we are the finest exclusive private clinic in this part of the state. But if you want to know the reason for the hospitalization, I am afraid I can't tell you."

"If it is a problem of doctor patient confidentiality, well, the rabbi is dead and it does not apply," I said.

"Oh, I know all that," she said tilting her head to the side very coyly. "They made all sorts of inquiries into the facilities and care schedule. They especially wanted to know if kosher food was available." She said this last with great disdain. As if Hannibal Lecter had asked for human flesh to be added to the spa menu.

"Is it?" asked Dafna.

Cathy was a bit perturbed by being interrupted, "Of course it is. We don't serve kosher right now because none of our clients have requested it. Our catering service is second to none. No, the reason I can't tell you is because the Kleins kept on insisting that they were inquiring for a third party and would not tell me the diagnosis. I assured them that we could handle the full range of psychiatric illnesses. But they never got back to me. What a shame."

Now, I knew why I was feeling such animosity coming from the lady. Good ole Cathy was broadcasting her inner feelings through her body language and general speaking tone. She was a dyed in the wool, chitlin eatin', Southern aristocratic bigot. She was pleased as punch that the Kleins never called back. Because if they had, she would have had to come up with some reason for turning down their request. Good ole' Cathy was not the marketing director of the spa. She was not responsible to get more patients into the facility. Her job was to be the gatekeeper. She was responsible for keeping certain undesirables out of the spa. My guess is, if you want to get in to Serenity Spa you had to be white, wealthy and from the right side of the tracks. Alcohol and prescription drug abusers were tolerated, but gays and hard drug addicts were out.

I was not gay, but I am sure that in Cathy's assessment I had more than one disqualifier working against me. My *yeshiva bocher* outfit certainly did not help.

What a smug old biddy.

"Did either of them seem to be ... more ... I don't know ... more concerned about the hospitalization?" I inquired.

"I understand what you're getting at," she said. "We get lots of people that ask about our facilities for a ..." — she held up her fingers like quotation marks — "... third party. But, I could not say if one of them was the candidate or not."

I turned to Dafna and said, "Well, I guess that's it. Do you have any more questions?"

"Yes, I do, Cathy," Dafna said with her own shit-kickin' grin spread across her face. "You know I am really impressed with what you folks do here. The brochure is so beautiful. Perhaps this would be the best place to move Dad." Dafna looked to me and said with a sad nod, "You know, his schizophrenia."

I decided to play along, "Oh yeah, his schizophrenia."

Cathy nodded her head seriously, "We handle schizophrenics all the time."

"Wonderful," said Dafna nodding her head imitating Cathy. "Money is no object. He's loaded. All his life, he put away a large chunk of his salary."

Cathy suddenly became all smiles, "Our clients' financial situation is never a consideration for acceptance in Serenity Spa."

Was her nose getting longer, or what?

"Just one little thing," added Dafna. "He keeps kosher ... really kosher."

"As I said, we have caterers," said Cathy her smile fading a bit.

"Good, good. And he'll need *Rosh HaShana* and *Yom Kippur* prayer services. That should not be a problem should it?"

"Well, I don't know ... ," stammered Cathy. "We have a non-denominational prayer room ..."

"That will be fine," declared Dafna. "His friends from the meat packing plant like to come by after they cash their checks on Fridays to drink beer and get drunk. That won't be a problem, will it?"

"I'm afraid we cannot ..." began Mrs. Paisley.

"I almost forgot," interjected Dafna. "His black boyfriend likes to come visit him occasionally. I assume your rooms are suitable for ... intimacy."

Mrs. Paisley's whole orderly world was crumbling before her, "I don't know about that ..."

Dafna asked, "Also, would it be all right if we could have a Passover *Seder* in your non-denominational prayer room. Just forty or fifty people. Close friends and family, you know."

"I don't know if we will be able ..." said Cathy in shock.

"Are patients allowed to smoke grass? You know ..." Dafna stopped and gave the marketing manager a big conspiratory wink, " ... for medicinal purposes."

"Are you referring to smoking marijuana ... here in Serenity Spa?" asked Mrs. Paisley having difficulty in forming the words.

"Why of course here. Dad loves a little pot every once in a while. He says it is good for his soul," said Dafna waxing philosophic.

"I ... I ... I ..." Cathy was at a loss for words.

"No need for an answer right now," said Dafna as she stood, pulling out a business card from her purse. "Here is my number. You let me know as soon as things are arranged. I'm sure that Dad will love it here," Dafna pulled my jacket and led me towards the door. "Remember, money is no object."

At the threshold, — I turned back, "Thank you, you have been most helpful."

Dafna added, "When you get things arranged give us call. We'll move Dad in the next day."

Mrs. Paisley sat dumbfounded at her desk.

∞

"Why did you do that?" I asked Dafna as we walked towards my car.

"Do what?" she asked in mock innocence.

"Make up that business about your dad. She nearly had a heart attack."

"That old hag is just a big phony. Did you hear her say 'the finest exclusive private clinic'?" asked Dafna, imitating Paisley in a commendable Southern drawl. "It made me sick," said Dafna in disgust.

I laughed and said, "Not as sick as she looked when you suggested smoking pot at a Passover *Seder* in Serenity Spa."

"Yes, I enjoyed that."

As we approached the car, Dafna bent over and said, "What's this?"

There was a cord coming out from under my car and she grabbed at it. When she pulled the cord, I heard a sound that I had not heard for nineteen years. Luckily, a sound that I had not forgotten.

Nineteen years earlier, I did my Marine Corps 'boot camp' in the San Diego Marine Recruit Depot. That was the most physically and mentally challenging period of my life. It was living hell and Staff Sergeant Frank Pansky, my drill instructor, was my designated devil. His job was to take the seventy five raw recruits of our platoon and at the end of thirteen weeks turn out as many raw Marines as he could. Many fell by the wayside. I suppose he was no more vicious than any of the other drill instructors except in one special area of training. It was common knowledge, that years before, he was held responsible for an incident in which a live grenade was accidentally dropped during grenade practice. Three recruits died and half a dozen were seriously injured. So, Sergeant Pansky decided this was never going to happen ever again to any of his boys. To accomplish this, he always went around with three or four blue practice M67 grenades in his pockets. At any time, in any place, day or night, whenever he thought it appropriate, he would pull out a grenade, pull the pin and then drop it on the floor. When we heard the sound of the spring mechanism pushing the spoon — the little lever at the side of the grenade — out of the grenade casing, we knew we had four seconds to scream 'Grenade!' and find cover. The practice grenades only went 'pfffft' and let out a small cloud of smoke, but if you were not at least fifteen feet away, Sergeant Pansky would dress you down so that you felt like you were one inch tall. He would scream in your ear telling you that you were now dead and buried, because you were too big a dunce to act quick enough. That your folks were now getting a telegram from the Department of Defense letting them know you were dead because you had been stupid and lazy. Then he would find appropriate punishment details. We got so we could recognize the sound of the spoon flying off the grenade in our sleep.

Thank you, Sergeant Pansky.

Because that was the sound I heard in front of Serenity Spa in Lansing. I heard that spoon fly off the grenade and I reflexively shouted, "Grenade!!!" Dafna was next to me and I pushed her down into a drainage ditch at the side of the gravel lot. She landed flat on her stomach and I fell right on top of her. Then we heard a loud explosion and debris rained down for about three or four seconds.

In my brain, I just repeated over and over 'Thank you Sergeant Pansky' so that after a while I was saying 'Pank you Sergeant Thansky'.

After the loud boom, my ears were ringing and there was an eerie silence. Maybe there just was no sound in the area or maybe my ears were not working yet. Eventually I was able to hear the people coming out of the clinic yelling and screaming, curious about what had occurred.

I got off of Dafna and helped her to her feet.

"Are you all right," I asked.

"Nothing injured as far as I can tell," she said. "What happened?"

"I assume it was an M67 offensive fragmentation grenade set as a booby trap under my car."

"A grenade? Your car?" she asked.

I pointed to my vehicle, "What is left of my car."

My GMC Terrain was never going to hit the 2,000 mile mark. The engine compartment was now scattered in a fifteen yard radius and the body of the vehicle looked like Swiss cheese. If we had been in that car, we never would have survived.

"How did they booby trap it?" she asked.

"My best guess is that someone taped the grenade under the car and then put a loop of string through the pin. They expected the string to snag on something as we drove and that would pull the pin. Without the pin, the spoon flies out and activates the four second fuse. If we were driving, I never would have heard the spoon fly out."

"You knew that there was a live grenade under the car because you heard the spoon fly out?" she asked incredulously.

"Well, yes I suppose I did," I said belittling the action.

"You saved my life. Oh my God. Thank you. Thank you so much."

"Don't thank me. Thank Sergeant Pansky."

CHAPTER FOURTEEN — *Mishagasin*

WE WERE SITTING AT Jumpin' Jack Slatterly's desk at the East Lansing Police Station filing a report about the car explosion. The state police were going to be officially in charge of the investigation because of the use of explosives. In addition, if it indeed turned out to be a grenade — and I am sure it was — the Feds would get into the action.

"Now I really am pissed," I said.

Jumpin' Jack said, "I understand completely. Someone is out to kill you and you just lost a new car."

"It's not that, the car was insured. I'm pissed because the state police hauled away the vehicle to their lab and they wouldn't let me take out the lunch hamper. I lost a great lunch," I said.

Dafna added, "And the case file and your laptop and the pictures."

I suddenly realized something else, "And my *tallis* and *tefillin*. They were in there too," I said with concern.

"Don't worry," said Slatterly. "I'll call the state guys and get the stuff back to you in a couple of days."

What would I use for tomorrow morning's prayer services? "Yeah, but I need them now."

"We'll make you another file, it will only take a couple of minutes," said Slatterly.

There was no reason that Jumpin' Jack would understand my concern, but Dafna apparently did. She said, "I'll lend you my husband's *tefillin*. They're just sitting at home in a drawer."

That was something very personal and I was moved, "Thank you."

"Hey, you saved my life. The least I can do is lend you *tefillin*," she said with a smile.

I had to say that Dafna was holding up pretty well. I saw how she handled herself yesterday after the mugging and now after the explosion.

Gutsy lady.

Slatterly asked, "When and where do you think they were able to rig the grenade?"

"Car was parked in the motel parking lot all night. That's when I would have done it," I said.

"So who knew you were staying at the Marriott?" the cop inquired.

"Dafna of course, Rabbi Lipsky, and *Rebbitzen* Klein. I think that's about it," I said.

"So that makes all of them suspects," said Slatterly.

Dafna was shaking her head from side to side. "I'm afraid it is not that simple," she said.

"Why not? Who else knew I was staying at the Marriott?" I asked.

"Just about everybody that has anything to do with the *kollel*," she answered.

"How do you know?" I asked.

"Because last night just about everybody that has anything to do with the *kollel* called me to find out about the mugging. They all knew about my kicking someone in the ... private parts. They knew about you and our investigation ... and they knew that you were staying at the Marriott."

I was confused, "Who told them?"

"My mother. She cooks, cleans, teaches, takes care of the house, and is the official busy body of the East Lansing *Kollel*. I even got a call from *Rebbitzen* Kalmonowitz."

I looked at Slatterly and said, "That means that everyone west of Detroit is a suspect."

"You know, I should run you out of town, like the sheriffs used to do in the Wild West," said Jumpin' Jack. "You are a regular crime wave. First the attempted armed robbery, now the car bombing. What is going on with you? Whose toes did you step on?"

"Somebody sure doesn't like me. But who? And why? So far, other than the stuff we told Julie this morning, we have come up with zip. Why would someone want to kill me?"

"Maybe it has nothing to do with the case," Dafna ventured.

"What do you mean?" I asked.

"You were a cop for fifteen years and a private investigator for two. You must have made enemies along the way. Maybe it is just payback time," said Dafna proud of her reasoning.

"You could be right," I said and then paused to look at the proud smile on Dafna's face. "But ... the odds are that you are not." Her smile faded considerably. "If we are talking about an enemy of mine from fifteen years ago, why did he wait so long for the payback and why come all the way out to Lansing? I don't work in this area and that means neither do my old enemies. It is just so much more likely that it is a new enemy. Someone from this case. So Slatterly's question is a good one. Whose toes did we step on? And what the hell did we uncover that is so secret that even we don't know we uncovered it?"

Dafna asked, "If the bomb was really a grenade, can't the police track down whoever placed it? You can't buy grenades in a grocery store."

"Honey, you are so wrong," said Slatterly. "Maybe, you can't buy them in a grocery store, but I can get you as many as you want down in Detroit. You live in the Appleby house don't you?" Slatterly asked Dafna.

"Yes, we bought the house from Mr. Appleby," she answered.

"He was one hell of a screwed up prepper," said Jumpin' Jack with a laugh. "Told everyone who would listen that we will be facing Armageddon any day now. You find any of his old prepper pals ... they'll be able to supply you with hand grenades. Anti-personnel mines, bazookas, even cannons. They're all nuts. That whole group has a regular underground army surplus supermarket. So, to answer your question ... just because we know it was a grenade ... and even if we are able to find out where and when it was stolen from the military ... does not mean that the state police will be able to find who planted the bomb."

"So you are just going to accept this?" asked an agitated Dafna. "Someone tried to kill you ... and me ... and you're not going to do anything?"

"Take it easy," I said trying to calm her. "Getting angry is not going to help. Look at the bright side of the thing."

"What bright side?" she asked in exasperation.

"If someone tried to kill us ... and it is connected to this case .... then we must be doing something right. Someone thinks we are getting too close for comfort and wants us out of the way," I answered.

Slatterly added, "Too bad you guys haven't got the foggiest idea what you might have discovered."

"There is that," I said. "Did you have to rub it in? Can't we just fool ourselves into thinking that we are super duper sleuths."

"Oh, yeah you guys are definitely super sleuths. I told the squad to pay attention to how you work so they can learn from you," said the cop sarcastically.

"Very funny," I said with a grin.

"Listen ... supercop ... someone is considering doing you bodily harm. I know you have a carry license ... are you packing?"

"I left my piece in Detroit, I did not think I needed a weapon," I answered.

"I can lend you something ... really ... it would make me feel better," said Slatterly.

"Is he going to give you a gun?" asked Dafna eagerly.

"Take it easy Annie Oakley," I told her. I turned to Jumpin' Jack and said, "Thanks for the offer. If I think a gun is necessary I will take you up on it."

"Take the gun," said Dafna.

"I don't want you anywhere near a firearm. No guns," I insisted.

"Let me see if the new copy of the case file is ready yet," said Slatterly as he left his desk to head for the copy machine.

"What do we do now?" she asked.

"We get the case file and then we wait for the loaner car from the insurance company," I said. "When I called the agency that damn agent had the nerve to say that he was not sure if my car was covered for getting blown up by a bomb. He only agreed to the loaner car when I threatened to go to his office and ram an M67 grenade up his *tuchis*."

Slatterly returned and threw a cardboard file on the table, "Here's the case file. Try not to get this one blown up," he said with a complacent smile. "Do you need a ride anywhere?"

"No, there's a loaner on the way."

"I don't know what's going on, but now I am also getting a gut feeling that maybe Rabbi Klein was not a simple suicide," said Slatterly. "That means, if someone did kill the Rabbi they are pretty shrewd. They think they got away with it. I hate that. I haven't got a shred of evidence to support my feeling. So, I am going to look at everything over and over again. I want the bastard. If you find anything, bring it to me. If you had cooperation up the whazoo before, now you're gonna get it up the super whazoo."

∞

Dafna and I were waiting just inside the main doors of the station. The agent said the car was on the way, but so far nothing in sight. She was scrolling though the messages on her phone and you could not tell that only a few hours ago she had almost been blown to bits.

Mrs. Dafna Lachler was an interesting lady.

What makes her tick?

"Has your mother always lived with you?" I asked.

"Actually, no. Just the past two years. My dad died suddenly about half a year before David. My mom was just shuffling around her big house in New York when David died. We knew I would need help with the girls, so she rented out her house and moved in with us. The arrangement is terrific. Since there is no Jewish school in the area we have been homeschooling the girls and Mom is an experienced teacher. She cooks, cleans, teaches, and cares for the girls. She loves it. The girls love her. And for me it couldn't be better."

"Especially the part where she allows you to go off galavanting around in an attempt to fulfill a childish wish to become a detective and almost getting yourself blown up," I said with a smile.

"Didn't I say it couldn't be better?"

"May I ask you one more question?"

"Sure ... we're partners ... that's what 'kick *tuchis*' partners are for."

"Just about everywhere I have been in the ultra-*frum* world, the separation between men and women is just about total. Now ... I'm not saying that I don't enjoy your company ... but how is it that you are allowed to be driving around with me or even sit with me?"

"You mean ... all alone ... like in a car," she added.

"Yeah, in a car."

"A parked car sometimes?"

"Exactly," I said.

"Okay, fair question," she began. "David once explained his ideas on the subject. What he said was that the whole men women separation issue is based on a two thousand year old conceptual argument between Rabbi Akiva and Rabbi Meir, two of the greatest Talmudic sages. You've heard of them, haven't you?"

"Of course," I answered. "Even I have heard of them."

"They both knew that there is a physical attraction between men and women and this can lead to all sorts of hanky panky ... if you know what I mean."

"I know what you mean."

"Rabbi Akiva appreciated the attractiveness of women and even encouraged it but he taught that a man must overcome any tendencies he had for indulging in hanky panky. Rabbi Meir, who was Rabbi Akiva's student, felt it was a lost cause. Once a man got a look at an attractive woman there was no way he was not going to indulge in hanky panky. His recommendation was that whenever women were in a situation where there were men that were not their husbands they had to cover up all that made them beautiful and attractive. You know … hair coverings, wigs, modest clothing. Better yet, they should never be in the company of men who were not their husbands. Possibly one of the factors that influenced Rabbi Meir was a bitter experience he had in this matter. His super intelligent wife committed adultery with one of the students in the *Yeshiva*. So Rabbi Akiva's rule for men is 'Look but don't touch' and Rabbi Meir's rule for men is 'Don't look'. And for women his rule is 'Don't allow the men to look'. The *frum* world leans towards Rabbi Meir's ruling."

"But you have been riding around with me for two days." I stated.

"I'll get to that," she said holding up an index finger. "You have to realize I am not your normal *frum* woman. I was raised in what is called a Modern Orthodox home. Many Modern Orthodox women do not cover their hair. I went to mixed youth groups — meaning boys and girls together. I was raised to know that a female can have male friends and vice versa, without there being unremitting orgies or hanky panky. I met David and was swept off my feet and then he swept me into the more stringent *frum* world of Detroit. It was quite foreign for me at first. I was eighteen when I married."

Wow so young. Even younger than I was. "You're parents were happy with that?"

"They did not have much to say about it."

"So you never went to college."

"Actually, I was in a special PhD program at the University of Michigan when I met David."

"At age seventeen?"

"No, I was sixteen."

"Sixteen? PhD?"

"I was a precocious kid," she said with a modest shrug of her shoulders.

"Where were your parents?"

"Back in New York. It was a perfect arrangement. We were here and they were in New York. They got along terrifically."

"Yeah, I can see how that would help."

"*Rebbitzen* Kalmonowitz was my savior. She helped me adapt to this strange new world that I was suddenly forced to live in. I also started my computer business and that required even more adaptation."

"Looks like you did all right."

"Yes and no," she said flopping her hand back and forth. "It was more like fifty percent I adapted and fifty percent they just tolerated my *mishagasin*."

Mishagasin was another expression I knew. *Meshuga* meant crazy, looney, off the wall. *Mishagasin* meant the expression of this craziness, strangeness, or weirdness. People were always using that expression when they referred to me.

"From what I've seen, the *frum* are not very tolerant," I commented.

"Yeah, they are. You just have to know how to play the game. Sort of like if you're crazy, they understand when you do strange stuff. After all, you're nuts, what do you expect?"

 "I get it. They say, 'She's Modern Orthodox … she doesn't know any better'."

"Sort of," she said rocking her head from side to side.

"And that is why you get to sit in a car with a man who is not your husband."

"That's only part of it. The main reason is because we are both unattached and prime wedding fodder. You know the expression that nature abhors a vacuum? Well, the Jewish community abhors unattached Jewish singles. Everyone is trying to match me off."

"So you date often?"

"I said they try. But the greater Lansing area is not rife with prime candidates to make an appropriate *shidduch*. So they will tolerate us sitting in the car because all of the *yentas* — rumor mongers — my mother included, are hoping that our little partnership turns into something more permanent."

Is she flirting with me?

Can't be.

It would not be a bad thing. I am actually having a good time.

Concentrate. You are on a case, no time for distractions.

I tried to return to what we were saying, "And that is why you do not cover your hair like all the other *frum* women."

Dafna cocked her head to the side and asked, "You think I don't cover my hair?"

"Well, yeah," I said looking at her long blonde pony tail.

"Thanks for the compliment," she said fingering her pony tail. "This is a *shaitel*."

Holy cow. It was a wig. I never would have guessed. "I had no idea."

"Just shows you, it pays to get good quality."

"I could have sworn you were a natural blonde," I said in surprise.

"Actually, this is my hair color, it is just not my own hair."

"It's really nice," I said complimenting her.

"Thank you, but as a *yeshiva bocher*, you really shouldn't have noticed."

"I know, but I could not help myself."

What did I just say?

Am I flirting with Dafna?

How inappropriate.

I have to watch myself.

CHAPTER FIFTEEN — PlayStation

THE LOANER WAS A fairly new red compact Hyundai and if you pushed the seat as far back as it would go it was adequate. Not comfortable ... but adequate. The car was not going to win any speed records but it was reliable transportation.

We both decided to officially end our investigatory day. Almost getting blown up seems to have that effect. Take it easy ... at least for today. Be happy you have a today.

It was decided that we should drive to Dafna's house. Four reasons shaped this decision. First, our clothes were smeared with dirt, engine oil and debris from my now defunct car. It was not that obvious on my black suit, but Dafna's outfit was ruined. Second, the state police were probably enjoying Mrs. Kalin's picnic lunch, but that did nothing to satiate the growing hunger pangs I was experiencing. I was starving and a late lunch at Dafna's house seemed very appealing. Third, I needed to pick up the *tallis* and *tefillin* that Dafna had so kindly promised me, so that I would have them for tomorrow morning's prayers. Fourth, and most important, Dafna said that there was a good chance that her computer programs had by now digested the material on the disks and it was quite possible that she could tell me what had been erased.

Mrs. Kalin went ballistic the moment she saw Dafna enter the house. But that was nothing compared to how she reacted when she heard that her daughter had nearly been blown into orbit. Then she really started to get angry. She calmed down only slightly when we were able to assure her that we had not been injured at all. Dafna's mom began a whirlwind of arguments aimed mainly at Dafna as to why she should stop all the 'detective nonsense'. She pointed out that what we were doing was obviously dangerous and Dafna had her two daughters to worry about.

Mrs. Kalin hit us with the four classic questions asked by any concerned Jewish parent when his or her child did something stupid. These questions had nothing in common with the four questions of the Passover *Seder*, but they were equally rooted in antiquity. Mrs. Kalin's four questions ... that she asked over and over ... were: 1 - Are you crazy? 2 - Are you out of your minds? 3 - Do you know what you are doing? 4 - *Bist du meshuga*?

The last was an earthy Yiddish expression that combined the meaning of the first three and challenged our basic ability to make rational decisions. Mrs. Kalin would say two sentences and then throw in one of the above questions to prove her point. Then she would start all over again.

A typical sequence of her sentences would be, 'You are going around asking people all sorts of things that make them angry. People who know how to make bombs. *Bist du mishuga*?'.

It took more than thirty minutes for her to concede that her daughter was indeed a grown woman and capable of making decisions on her own — no matter how irrational they were. So, it was not until almost an hour had passed that Mrs. Kalin relented in her harangue and

Dafna was able to go change her clothes. It then gave Dafna's mom the opportunity to offer me a late lunch/early supper, which I kindly accepted.

She is a terrific cook.

When Dafna returned to the kitchen she was wearing a bright yellow T-shirt and tan skirt. She wore a *tichel* — head scarf — rather than a wig and I could see a few wisps of her own hair sticking out. It really was the same color as her *shaitel*. Interesting. It was also the first time that I had a hint of Dafna's figure. Not bad. Not bad at all.

There I go, once again, making observations that were inappropriate for a *yeshiva bocher*, but I couldn't help it. I said I was a good detective, didn't I?

I had second helpings of just about everything Dafna's mom served and was feeling sated and sublime. I would have taken thirds and maybe a fourth helping, but I did not want them to think I was a *chazir* — pig. It was not often that I had food as good as this. Well fed and in the after-effects of the adrenaline rush of this morning's excitement, I just wanted to sit back and do nothing for a while.

I was knocking at the entrance to Nirvana when Dafna asked, "Do you want to go to the Vault?"

The computer disks.

Of course I did. Maybe they contained the reason for someone blowing my car to smithereens.

"Absolutely," I answered getting to my feet.

"Let's go," she said.

∞

Dafna sat in front of a computer console and began typing. Well, I guess she was typing because her fingers flew across the keyboard in a blur and words and symbols appeared on the screen. There was some whirring and line after line started rolling up the screen.

"Aha," said Dafna.

Her practiced eye had seen something that had come up on the screen, but to me it was all gibberish. "Aha, what?" I asked.

Dafna pointed to the screen, "Someone definitely did a Google swipe of the disk."

"When was it done?" I asked.

Dafna checked something on the screen and said, "Two days before the rabbi died at 7:23 in the evening."

"Not so great," I commented.

"Why?"

"That means that four people could have done the swipe," I said stating the obvious. "Rabbi Klein, *Rebbitzen* Klein, someone with access to the computer who killed the rabbi, or someone with access to the computer who did not kill the rabbi. It could be anyone. In addition we still don't know if the erased files had anything to do with Rabbi Klein's death. Please tell me you can tell me what was in those files," I said to Dafna beseechingly.

She looked at me and asked, "Do you want the good news or the bad news first?"

"Why do you always play these games with me? Just tell me and put me out of my misery."

"Okay, here goes. I can't tell what was in those files ..." she paused for effect.

"Stop it already, you're killing me."

"I can't tell you what was in those files ..." she repeated and then continued, " ... right now. Because they have been erased completely and overwritten, so they are gone ... gone .... gone. But from the signature on the disk I know that these files were downloads from the internet and where they came from. I can get them. It's going to take a few hours and quite a bit of computer magic and finesse, but I am pretty certain I will be able to tell you what was in most of those files."

"*Brook Hashem* — praise be to God." I knew my pronunciation was terrible. It should have come out *Bah - ruchhh Hah- shem*, but it was the closest I could get.

Dafna shook her head from side to side, "You have got to practice that 'ch' sound some more. You made God into a babbling brook. The Hashem brook."

She got back to typing and setting her computer in action. I could not help but wonder how she did what she did so successfully.   "How long have you been a computer nerd?"

She continued writing her program as she spoke, never taking her eyes off the screen, "I suppose it started when I was six or seven ..."

"Six years old?" I exclaimed.

"I started reading at age three. So, yeah, six. That's when my dad bought me my first computer."

"Who taught you to do what you do?" I asked.

"Mostly self taught," she answered simply. "Computer language and writing code just came naturally to me. At first I had no idea what I was doing so I just played around. Within a month I wrote my first program."

Something was bothering me, "How come you can find this data and the East Lansing computer guy cannot?"

"Remember I told you that I don't really read?"

"Yeah, you said it had something to do with image processing."

"Exactly," she agreed. "Well, I am able to do the same thing with my computer. It does not read the data, it looks for the image of the data. Just like I do in my brain. To do this I use what is known as 'parallel processing'."

"So this 'parallel processing' is special?" I asked.

Dafna chuckled, "Yeah, you could say that."

"So why don't the other computer geeks use parallel processing?"

"A couple of reasons," she said. "First some geek has to write the code to do the parallel processing."

"I get it," I said. "They don't know how, but you do. Is that it?"

"I suppose there are a couple thousand people who could write code for 'parallel processing'," she stated simply.

"In the country?" I asked.

"In the world," she said. "But that is not enough. To use 'parallel processing' you also need tremendous computer capacity. Like a super computer. NASA has a set up. The credit card companies also have one. It's very expensive."

"And you have a super computer?"

"No, I don't. The Cray Company, the builder of the super computers, went out of business years ago."

"So, how do you make it work," I inquired.

"I improvise," she said pointing to a three foot stack of electronic hardware sitting on the table located in the middle island. "You see those machines? Read what it says on them."

I could see letters embossed on the top surface of the uppermost machine, "Sony - PS4"

"That is a Sony PlayStation4. Its brain is the Jaguar. It has the most advanced multi-core system that can be found in the world. The CPUs are just about the quickest in the world, but that is nothing compared to the GPUs. That's what does it."

"I once heard something about CPUs, but what are GPUs?"

"Graphics Processing Units," said Dafna, surprised at my ignorance. "It's the GPUs that give the unit its oomph. They can change all the pixels on the screen tens and even hundreds of times a second."

"Is this machine anything like my niece's ... PlayStation?"

"The very same," she said.

"Are you saying that 'parallel processing' is some sort of game?"

"No, not at all. What I did there was wire twelve PS-4 machines together. That's my creation and that is what I use instead of a super computer and that is why I can do 'parallel processing' and the other geeks cannot."

"And this super PlayStation is going to get us the missing files?"

Dafna hit the last key with gusto. She pressed the 'enter' key and watched the material written on the screen race upward, "There, I'm done."

"Did the computer get the files?" I asked eagerly.

"Oh no, the super PlayStation does not get files. It only finds them," she said.

"So how will we find out what is in the files?"

"I'm going to borrow them from where they originated."

"Explain please."

"Those files originally came into the computer as files downloaded from the internet. They are no longer on the computer but I know their origin. I will simply go to the site that sent the files and download another copy."

"Why do these sites let you come into their computers and make copies of their files?" I asked.

"They don't. As a matter of fact, the sites are usually fairly well protected so that people cannot see their files at all."

"So, how do you get permission to enter their sites?"

"I don't ..." was all she said.

It took me a moment and then I understood. "I think I really don't want to know how you do this."

Dafna nodded her head and said, "I think that would be best."

"Yeah," I agreed. "That would be best."

"I've got a lot of work ahead of me tonight. Why don't you take the *tallis* and *tefillin*, and head over to the *kollel* for afternoon prayers then go back to your hotel for a good night's sleep. I'll see you tomorrow morning for breakfast."

"Is your mother cooking?" I asked eagerly.

"Mom's cooking," she said.

"I'll be here."

∞

Almost getting killed has a way of exhausting you and when I returned to the Marriott after prayer services, I was ready to turn in early. I had just finished my shower when the room phone rang. I was quite surprised to hear Rabbi Kalmonowitz's voice say, "*Reb* Shimon, are you all right? I heard about your car. It's a *nase* — miracle — no one was hurt."

"I'm fine *Rebbi* , not a scratch on me," I assured the rabbi.

"And Dafnaleh, is she all right?"

How did he know about her?

Of course ... Mrs. Kalin.

"We're both fine," I said.

"You know what this means?" asked the rabbi rhetorically. "It is as I said. This was not a suicide. Someone killed Rabbi Klein."

I did not want to point out that there were other possibilities that would explain the car bomb explosion. Because for some reason what the rabbi just said suddenly rang true to me.

You can take it to the bank.

I don't know what caused me to have that sensation. It was something in Rabbi Kalmonowitz's tone. So, I answered, "You are probably right."

"I am definitely right," insisted the rabbi.

Rabbi Kalmonowitz's roots were from a *misnaged yeshiva* … and that meant that he was not one that believed that certain rabbis had miraculous abilities. His official credo was that in times of need, each person should pray directly to God and not rely upon spiritual go-betweens. Nevertheless, it was rumored around the *yeshiva* that *Rebbi* could do stuff. If he prayed for you, the prayers got answered. Sick people got well. Business problems suddenly were solved. And much much more.

If Rabbi Kalmonowitz says it was murder … you could not ignore it.

"Yes, *Rebbi*, I am working on it."

"Tell me what you have learned so far," he requested.

I spent the next half hour giving the rabbi all the details of the investigation.

Rabbi Kalmonowitz ended the conversation with, "Let me know how things progress and keep up the good work. Also, get some sleep."

CHAPTER SIXTEEN — *Surveillance*

THE NEXT MORNING I was back at Dafna's home accepting my third fluffy onion cheese omelet. I was trying my darndest to refuse Mrs. Kalin's continuous offerings, but I was not succeeding.

She was one heck of a cook.

I think I had three — maybe four — hot buttered bagels and I had downed I don't know how many cappuccinos. Dafna's mom was now cutting me a nice large slab of chocolate cake for dessert.

I have never eaten food as good as this in my life. My mom was a firm believer that a nutritious diet for our family was made up of equal parts frozen, takeout and restaurant food. She never cooked. All the holidays and parties were always catered. The food in the Marines was always decent but never really good. Bethany was a total disaster in the kitchen and considered it a major success if she was able to cook pasta or scorch some toast. After my marriage went *kaput,* I was on my own and I have to admit that I am a total boor when it comes to things culinary. For the most part I had reverted back to my mother's food formula to obtain the nutrients to maintain my bodily functions.

This was totally different.

I don't think I am going to be able to get up from the table.

I was now enjoying Mrs. Kalin's triple chocolate cake as we waited for Dafna to show. Apparently she had had a very long night and was still getting dressed. Her mom kept up a constant one-sided chatter demonstrating that she indeed was the official busy body of the greater Lansing area Jewish community.

Dafna stumbled in at about 8:30 am, yawning as she entered. She was back to her *shaitel* and wore a loose fitting burgundy blouse over a long black skirt. Her figure was now totally hidden as per the rules of *tznius*— modesty.

Too bad.

"Coffee ... now ... please," was all she could say as she flopped into a chair.

Mrs. Kalin prepared her a cup and set it before her.

"Any luck?" I asked.

"You mean in finding the files?"

"Yes."

"I got most of them," she said taking a gulp from her cup.

"So what were they? What was in them?" I asked eagerly.

"Not now," she said shaking her head.

"Why not?"

Dafna held up her right hand to hide her left index finger that was pointing to her mom. Mrs. Kalin was washing dishes with her back to us but it was obvious that she was straining not to miss a single word of our conversation.

"I agree with you. I think that's a good idea," I said.

"Once I finish another cup of this elixir of life, we'll go down to the Vault and I'll show you."

∞

When we were safely ensconced in Dafna's work area, she handed me a stack of papers. "These are the printouts of the files that were wiped. To save you time I will tell you that they are credit card statements from eight different companies, going back seven years, twenty-four statements in all. The Klein family, and that means Devorah Klein, bought just about everything you can imagine online and offline with her credit cards. This was not a revelation because I already knew that Devorah did not like to touch money. She considered it icky and full of germs from all the people who touched it before her. So it was always a credit card or check."

"Yeah, I could see that would fit *Rebbitzen* Klein," I agreed.

"That also means that there were an average of fifty seven items charged to each one of the cards. Almost five hundred charges a month. That includes all her bills and the stuff she bought online and a cup of coffee or a newspaper or a parking charge, the smallest of things."

"Why are you telling me this?"

"Because I assumed that whoever erased these statements did not want us to find particular credit card charges."

"That makes sense."

"That means one or more of the items on these particular statements is a charge that does not appear on any of the statements that remained on the disk. Do you follow me?" she asked.

"Yeah, I do. Because if they had appeared on the other statements they would have been erased as well."

"Exactly," she said with a smile. "So, what I had to do was get all the statements from all the companies for the past seven years and then compare them with the erased statements to find which items were unique."

"Did you say five hundred charges a month?"

"Yup,"

"That sounds like a lot of work," I commented.

Dafna let out a deep yawn, "Tell me about it."

"And ..."

She handed me a single sheet of paper with a single item on it. "After I eliminated one-time charges like a payment of a parking fee, or a cup of coffee and the like, I came up with twenty-four charges of around $300 a piece to Doctor George Felix. His fee started at $250 but over the years went up to $375."

"What kind of doctor is he?"

"Psychiatrist."

"Oh ho," I said in surprise. "What were the charges for? For a treatment? Per hour?"

"Can't tell. The doctor's records are not on his computer. I suspect he has an external disk. I can only get at those records for the short periods the disk is connected to the computer. For now if we want to know why the rabbi was seeing him we are going to have to ask him," she answered.

"Doesn't that seem strange? Someone is trying to hide these visits to a psychiatrist. But why go to all that bother and then leave all the brochures from the psychiatric clinics in the desk?"

"Don't have a clue," said Dafna with a shrug of her shoulders.

"The Kleins didn't have any kids, maybe that was the reason. But then again, if they went there for reasons related to infertility, why did they have to erase this information?" I asked.

"I don't know yet. But the moment Dr. Felix connects his external disk my little program will slip in and voila. Unfortunately, no connect until now."

"I told you I don't want to know how you are violating half a dozen federal laws. Officially, you never told me anything," I stated.

"No problem," she said with a knowing smile. "What's up for today, besides the appointment to see the director of the Hillel House at two o'clock? We got mugged two days ago and bombed yesterday. You got something to top that?" she joked.

"Rabbi Kalmonowitz called me last night," I said gravely.

"The whole world called me last night. Everyone heard about the bomb. I was on the phone until midnight. I didn't get started with the computers until they finished pestering me. Why do you think I'm so tired?"

"*Rebbi* is more convinced than ever that someone killed Rabbi Klein."

"Did it sound like he knows something he was not telling you?" ventured Dafna.

"Exactly," I said.

"I told you … money in the bank," said Dafna with a nod of her head. "So, what are we going to do?"

"Well, for starters we have to look at this case differently. Up until now we have been trying to see if Rabbi Klein committed suicide and why he might have done it. Let's just assume it was murder. To solve this case we need to find the motive and the method. Because whoever did it made sure that it looked like the rabbi took his own life."

"How do we do that?" asked Dafna.

"First off, assume nothing. We will take it as a fact that everyone is a suspect except the rabbi himself. Next we have to go through these suspects one by one and eliminate those who could not possibly be the murderer."

"Excuse me," said Dafna holding up a questioning palm. "The last time I looked, we did not have any suspects."

"I know," I said. "From now on, everyone is a suspect. Alibis have to be checked because you can assume the killer is lying to you."

"What do you mean, 'Everyone is a suspect'?" asked Dafna. "You think Rabbi or *Rebbitzen* Lipsky could have done it?"

"I don't think they did, but that does not mean they did not," I said firmly. "The police never treated this as a murder, so it was never really investigated looking for a killer.   So that means everyone.   That includes the Lipskys, all the *bocherim* in the *kollel* and their wives, *Rebbitzen* Klein, just for starters. Once we finish with the people closest to the Rabbi, we look farther afield."

"You have got to be kidding," said Dafna hopefully.

"Not at all. Next we have to figure out the method. If he did not hang himself, how was the rabbi killed? That means we have to talk to the medical examiner. The alarm was operational at the time of the crime so how did the murderer circumvent the system? Finally, how did the murderer get to the crime scene and then escape undetected. One of the neighbors down the street has a surveillance camera that shows that only four vehicles came down the street during the time the rabbi died and none stopped to discharge or take on passengers."

"The murderer could have walked there," suggested Dafna.

"Not in East Lansing. Everyone drives except for the exercise nuts. Anyone walking or running would be stopped by the police. Besides they would have shown up on the surveillance tape."

"Maybe they didn't stop on the rabbi's street," offered Dafna.

"What good would that do them?"

"Well, if they stopped, say a block away and came through the backyards, we would never see them," said Dafna stating the obvious.

Why hadn't I thought of that?

"Can you find us some more surveillance cameras? A lot of people have become security conscious. Is there a listing of security cameras in the area?" I asked.

"Not really, but I have an idea."

With that she turned to her console and began typing. "What are you doing?" I asked.

"If the camera is on a closed internal system, then it will take forever to find all the cameras in the area, if at all. But some people have their cameras hooked to their smart phones, so the owners can see what is happening even if they are far away. Most of those will go through a cable/internet server. There are only a few in this area. I'm just going to take a look to see if anyone near the Klein house is broadcasting."

"More image recognition," I said showing off.

"Nice," she said with a knowing smile. "We'll make you into a computer nerd before you know it. "

A few minutes went by and the screen suddenly showed a picture of someone's backyard. After a moment the picture changed to show a side yard and this was followed by a front lawn. Dafna pointed to the screen, "This is from a surveillance system on the street directly behind the Klein's home and four houses North. What you are seeing is a live feed from the various cameras."

"We don't need to see what is going on now, we have to see what happened back then."

"I know," said Dafna. "I'm working on it. Give me a second."

The screen changed to a night scene and the time legend at the bottom of the screen showed it was the night that

Rabbi Klein died. At first there was no pedestrian or motor vehicle traffic that were relevant so Dafna fast forwarded until there was something to study. Then, about twenty minutes before the rabbi's estimated time of death a white car came down the street and stopped at the house directly behind the Klein house. The image was poor and taken from a great distance but there was no question that someone got out of the vehicle and went into the side yard. Forty seven minutes later, a person could be seen leaving that same yard and climbing into the vehicle. The car made a u-turn and left the street.

"Did you just see what I saw?" I asked.

"That's our murderer," said Dafna.

"Good chance," I said. "Detective Lachler, congratulations. We are on our way to solving this case. Make me a copy of the surveillance tape. Also what is the address of the house with the surveillance camera?" I inquired.

"392 Division. What do you need the address for?"

"I have to go see Slatterly. We need his help to find that car. And he needs to make an official request for this surveillance tape."

"I'm confused. You already have the tape," she said.

"Yes, but it was obtained ... by someone who shall remain nameless ... illegally."

"So, you are just going to leave me here? We're partners."

"Take the computer disks back to Slatterly so that he can return the computers to *Rebbitzen* Klein. Get a couple of hours of sleep. I'll be back to take you to our two o'clock meeting at the Hillel House."

"What do you expect to find there?"

"Maybe the reason Rabbi Klein was killed," I said seriously.

CHAPTER SEVENTEEN — Postmortem

I SHOWED SLATTERLY THE video and after conferring with Julie Dalton they agreed to check out the car. Even with all their video enhancement techniques they could not see anything more than a 2009 Chevrolet and that its color was white. The license plate was unreadable and all they could say about the person getting out of the car was that he was somewhere between five and six feet tall, wearing dark clothes and a dark hat.

That really narrowed it down.

The cops pointed out to me that all I had was a white car stopping on the street behind the rabbi's house around the time that the rabbi died and that someone came and left. There was no evidence of any criminal activity on the video, but coupled with the bombing of my car, they agreed it could not be ignored.

Jumpin' Jack called Dr. Anthony Slocomb, the county medical examiner and he agreed to meet with me that morning.

Ingham County did not fund a separate medical examiner's office, instead these services were supplied by contract through a private corporation, Laurel Forensic Pathology. Dr. Slocomb was the chief and he would call in other pathologists if the work load got heavy.

Their offices were located in a modern two story building surrounded by well landscaped grounds. I parked in one of the marked visitor spots and the receptionist directed me to Dr. Slocomb's office.

Slocomb was in his early sixties and his full head of silver grey hair was combed straight back. He was about my size but getting heavy in the gut and wore a long white lab coat over a blue shirt. No tie. His desk was neat and he had Rabbi Klein's file open in front of him.

After the formality of the greeting handshakes and name exchanges, he sent his secretary to prepare the coffee he had requested for both of us, "What can I do for you?"

I always found talking with forensic pathologists tricky. On the one hand, they were super eager to help. Many of them were dedicated to catching the guilty and freeing those wrongly accused. The problem was that they did not like dumb detectives telling them that they were wrong. Slocomb had signed off on the Klein case with the diagnosis of 'probable suicide'. Now I was coming along and spitting in his eye.

Choosing my words carefully, I said, "I'm here because we think there is a good chance that Avraham Klein was not a suicide."

"What is the basis for that theory?" he wanted to know.

Naturally I did not say, 'Rabbi Kalmonowitz says so'. Instead I mentioned the *negel vasser* and lack of a urine puddle. Then I added the car bombing incident and the recent discovery of the white car. He listened carefully, thought for a moment and then said, "Fair enough."

I have no idea what he meant by that.

"Do you know how to strangle people?" he asked.

After all my military and police training, if there was anything I did know how to do, it was to strangle people. "Yeah, I think I do," I said proudly.

"Okay, how does strangling kill people? Do you break their neck? Keep them from breathing? Block the blood supply to the brain?"

"I suppose, it could be all three."

"Absolutely correct. We do high resolution CT's on the bodies now. We are not worried about the high x-ray doses, because after all it isn't going to kill them. Ha, ha," said the doctor chuckling over his timeworn joke. "The images we obtained — in this case the victim's body and neck — allowed us to see the crushing of the trachea and soft tissues. His neck was not broken or else we would have seen a hangman's fracture or some other bony injury. Instead, intense force was employed to block the intake of air and the flow of blood. He lost consciousness and then died. This was not done with someone's hands or we would have seen the evidence. It was a thin rope tied around his neck. What we call a ligature strangling."

"I am sure you are leading up to something," I stated.

"Just this, if this was not a suicide by hanging then someone strangled him using a great amount of force. Much more than the standard strangulation," said the doctor.

"You mean with their hands?" I asked.

"No, no. I already said definitely not with the hands. The tissue injury is inconsistent with manual strangulation. Some instrument was used. By instrument I mean a rope or a wire."

"Like an old fashioned garrote," I offered.

"Similar, but as I said before the large amount of tissue injury is more consistent with a hanging. When someone dies by hanging, the body weight is concentrated on the rope encircling the neck. To get that much injury with a garrote you would need a very powerful individual or some sort of contraption that could exert such a force for an extended period of time."

"And no contraption was found at the scene," I said.

"Take a look at these photos," said the doctor.

Slocomb showed me pictures of the rabbi's neck without the rope taken from several angles. There were also some pictures taken in the Kleins' basement with the rope in place. I was not sure what he wanted me to see, so I just began, "There is a rope around the rabbi's neck and I see the marks left by the rope. That's about it."

"Absolutely correct. That's it. That's all we found. There was some trauma to the heels, but other than that all we have are these marks. He died by strangulation. What I'm saying is that I made my call that this was a suicide based on the fact that there was no evidence that it was not."

"But now there is," I stated.

"Not exactly evidence, but enough to make me suspicious," he said with a nod. "So, now let's look at the marks on the neck, thinking this may not be a suicide."

"How does that change anything?"

"Look at this part of the neck, do you notice that the mark here is wider than it is at the front or here in the back?"

I had not noticed the difference before but after he pointed it out it was obvious, "Now that you mention it, yeah."

"Such a widening could occur if the rope slips as the body sags with death. But ... it could also occur because someone strangled the victim, then removed the instrument used to strangle them and replaced it with a rope around the neck and then hung the body. That way we would have the marks from the instrument that killed him and then the new marks from the hanging."

"Could you tell the difference?" I asked.

"Easily, because each causes a different pattern of tissue injury. One would have been inflicted when the victim was still alive and the other after death. But I can only see those differences if the marks were separate. Because they laid one over the other I couldn't tell which was which."

"Was there anything else that was unusual in this case?"

"Now that you ask, there was," said Slocomb. "The rope used was a specialty nylon reinforced cord. You can buy it at any maritime supply store. It's stuff used on boats ... very strong. What is unusual is that most suicides use a heavier rope. Manila or sisal or something synthetic. But definitely something thicker. 10 mm or 3/8th inch stuff. The cord that was used is strong enough but it is also extremely thin. I think we measured it at 4 mm. That's about 1/8th of an inch.   Not your typical choice for suicide."

"So you now think this case is a homicide?" I asked.

The doctor shook his head, "No, not at all. All I'm saying is that it could be. If you find a device that could have been used to strangle him, I might be willing to go out on a limb."

∞

I left Laurel with the intention of checking out another of the private psychiatric clinics when I got a call from the secretary at the Hillel House, "You have an appointment with Susan Silverman at two. Unfortunately Susan has to leave town this evening and can't do two o'clock. If you could make it to the Hillel House by one, we will fit you in. Otherwise we will have to reschedule for next week."

Something told me that we just might find the motive for the rabbi's death at the Hillel House and I was not going to wait until next week, "I'll be there at one."

I called Dafna and told her about the change in schedule and that I was on the way over to pick her up.

The Lester & Jewell Morris Hillel Jewish Student Center was located just off the MSU campus and was a home away from home for the Jewish students who attended the university. The building had numerous multi-purpose rooms, a small restaurant, and a dining room. Activities were organized for all the Jewish holidays and they even made kosher meals available for the students on the Sabbath and other holidays. They had an executive staff of fifteen and a maintenance staff of another ten. Susan Silverman was in the executive office space just to the right of the main door.

After a twenty minute wait we were shown into her office and found her sitting behind her desk speaking on the phone. She motioned for us to take seats while she finished her call. Susan Silverman looked to be about fifty years old. She was wearing a white blouse sheer enough to make out the pattern of her lace bra. There was a long strand of pearls around her neck and she had matching pearl earrings. Her blonde tinged brown hair was parted in the middle and styled sort of like a helmet. It was cropped short in the back and gradually became longer towards the front. She was speaking angrily to a supplier who was not coming through with the goods promised for the next day. The supplier was adequately admonished, verbal assurances were given, and they ended their conversation hoping that things would work out to their mutual satisfaction.

"What can I do for you?" asked Susan cheerfully.

"I'm a private investigator and my name is Sy Lincoln, and this is ..."

"Dafna Lachler. Oh, I know who you are," interrupted Susan. "You are the two that nearly got blown up yesterday."

"How did you know?" I asked.

"East Lansing is a pretty small town. How many *yeshiva bocherim* get blown up in this town? You're celebrities. You're famous."

Dafna added, "I could live without the fame."

Pointing at Dafna she said, "They said on the news that the day before you kicked some guy in the groin. I bet you taught him a thing or two."

"I certainly learned something," said Dafna.

"What?" asked Susan.

"Wear heavier shoes."

Susan laughed and then said, "OK what did you want to discuss?"

"We are investigating the death of Rabbi Klein and we understand that he counseled some of the students here at the Hillel House," I said.

All the mirth faded from Ms. Silverman's face and she said dourly, "Why didn't you say you wanted to talk about Rabbi Klein? It would have saved us some time and bother."

"What do you mean?" I inquired.

Susan stated quite officially, "The Hillel House Center does not wish to comment on anything to do with Rabbi Klein. That's what our lawyers advised us to say."

"What's going on here? Why all this lawyer double talk?" asked Dafna.

"That's the script the lawyers wrote and that is our official policy," said Susan angrily. "Now off the record I will tell you that I want nothing to do with that witch ever again. If she ever steps foot in this building I will have her arrested and we will prosecute her to the full extent of the law. If I could, I would rather just take her out back and personally kick the ... well, you know what ... out of her."

I had no idea what she was talking about and from the look on Dafna's face neither did she.

I held up a palm to stop the ranting of the executive secretary of the Hillel House, "Could you tell me who you are talking about? Whose *tuchis* do you want to kick?"

"Mrs. Klein's, of course," stated Susan vehemently. "She is a monster. How she talked. And she is supposed to be the wife of a rabbi."

"Do you mean Devorah Klein? Who was married to Rabbi Avraham Klein?" asked Dafna.

"The very same," said Susan.

"Obviously, she must have done something to make you this angry. Could you share it with us?" I inquired.

"I don't care what the lawyers said, I will be glad to tell you," said Ms. Silverman. "About six weeks ago she made an appointment to see me. When she came here she sat in that very chair, straight as a ramrod, and claimed that one of the female students being counseled by her husband had seduced him and had turned him against her. She said it with such vehemence and intensity that it was downright scary. She cursed this entire organization, our efforts, the people who work here, and especially me."

Using inappropriate language seemed highly unusual for *Rebbitzen* Klein, "She used swear words?"

"No," said Susan. "No swear words. She said that she was going to use her 'powers' to place a curse on everyone associated with our organization. She also said that she would take us to court and sue us. Me personally and the entire Hillel organization."

"I'm sure people come to you all the time with all sorts of accusations about ... I don't know what." I said. "What made Mrs. Klein's accusation so different."

"The way she said it," said Susan. "As if she was going to invoke all the black arts in the world to see me destroyed. That lady broadcasted evil and I felt threatened. Really threatened. Like she really was going to do something violent."

"Did she? Do anything violent?" I asked.

"No, she sat there and barely moved a muscle but her tone was frightening," said Ms. Silverman emotionally.

"I have to ask this. Was there any truth to what she said?"

"At the time I had no idea. There was always the possibility that something like that could occur. But since then, we have investigated the claim extensively and we were convinced ... absolutely convinced ... that it was not true. All of the students he counseled male and female assured us that the rabbi always acted super proper. All meetings were in public places. We contacted our insurance carrier and their risk management group sent an investigator and his report also found no signs of impropriety."

"Who was the investigator?" I asked.

"I think his name was Frank or Franklin Diangus or something," she answered.

"Frank DeAngelo?" I ventured.

"That's it," agreed Susan.

"Short fellow with a limp?" I added.

"I don't know if you would consider him short. He was about my height. But, yes, that sounds like him," she said.

"Do you know him?" Dafna asked me.

"'Angel' Frank, was the assistant chief of detectives when I first started on the squad. He retired a half dozen years ago. Terrific cop," I said.

Susan got up from her desk and went to a file cabinet. She opened the drawer and found a file and extracted a packet of papers, "Here is an extra copy of his report. It is very extensive. You can keep it," she said.

I took the report and flipped through the pages, "That's Frank for you."

I quickly read the end of the report and there was no doubt that Frank was convinced that there was no credence to Mrs. Klein's claims that the rabbi was involved with any of the students or staff, female or male.

"So what happened after that?" asked Dafna.

"Did you contact the police?" I asked.

"No," she said.

"Why not?"

"I liked Rabbi Klein," said Ms. Silverman. "He helped many of our students. As a matter of fact he was involved with three students that were diagnosed with suicidal tendencies. In addition to the psychological help that they received from the mental health clinic, the rabbi talked to them about the Jewish belief that forbids taking your own life. The students all said that Rabbi Klein was most understanding and had helped them very much. It was very surprising to hear that he took his own life."

"I have a feeling that was not the end with his wife, was it?" I said.

"No. Two days later, I received a voicemail," said Susan. "I recognized Mrs. Klein's voice immediately. Her message was 'You are going to pay'. Really ... really creepy. I called our lawyers and they said our options were limited. If we did anything there would be a huge public relations problem. How would it look for the Hillel House to be in a legal battle with one of the respected rabbis of the community? So they set up the script and we have no official comment on anything to do with the Kleins. But personally I hope she rots in hell."

Ms. Silverman was not overly fond of the *rebbitzen*.

This was a new revelation.

Devorah Klein was not always the proper and refined *rebbitzen*.

What triggered her to behave so?

CHAPTER EIGHTEEN — Jihad

WHEN WE EXITED THE Hillel House offices we were surprised to see a group of some fifty Arab protestors gathered at the base of the steps in front of the building entrance. Their signs said that they were demonstrating against Israel's oppression of the Palestinian people. There was not much of an Israeli presence in East Lansing, so they apparently decided to protest in front of the Jewish Hillel House. Some of the girls wore the *hijab* and some of the guys a checkered *kafiyeh*. A few held up signs that supported the Palestine cause but most just milled about chanting Arabic slogans.

Which I did not understand.

They seemed quite zealous and ticked off about something.

Isn't America great?

The right to gather and protest is the backbone of American democracy. If these guys want to demonstrate, I was not going to interfere. They had every right to be here and that meant that I had to keep my mouth shut and move on.

I am not a Zionist. Meaning, I did not believe that the only future for the Jewish people, after 2,000 years of Diaspora, was to emigrate in order to go build up our homeland. I was not for or against those that believed in this credo. The reason for my wishy-washy stance was because I am almost totally ignorant when it came to things dealing with Israel. I had never been exposed to the subject because until recently I barely knew anything about Judaism. All my studies taught me that for Jews the land of Israel was holy. Not just special, but inherently holy. The city of Jerusalem was holier still. You even had to make a special blessing when you stepped on the soil of the Holy Land for the first time. But that was the limit of my knowledge about Israel. One day I might go to visit the Holy Land but that was way in the future.

I had even less information regarding the Israeli government's internal and external politics and I was not really up to date with the Arab-Israel conflict and the Palestinian question. As with all disputes I knew that there were two sides to the coin, but I had no idea about Zionist doctrine and I knew even less about the Palestinian side of the argument. Before I would take any position on this issue I would have to get some accurate info. Until I was better informed, I would just keep my mouth shut on the whole topic.

However, there was one thing that I did know.

The new "anti-Israel" movement was the old "anti-Semite" movement in new garb.

As I said, I am far from being an expert in this field but from the little that I heard on the radio and TV, I knew that the 'anti-Israel' movement was based quite a bit on false information and outright lies. In their rhetoric, Jews were never referred to as 'Jews', they were called Zionists. The Zionist government discriminates against its Arab citizens and practices apartheid. Every Zionist was a racist. Every Zionist was a world destroying oppressor.

Sound familiar?

You never heard the word 'Jew' at the anti-Israel demonstrations, but who were they kidding?

People like Captain Flowers came in all sorts of shapes and sizes.

So, if there was any group that did not get my sympathy it was this group. But I would allow them to practice their basic right of protest and I would get out of their way. I directed Dafna to the side so that we would skirt around the angry crowd and get to our car.

Dafna pointed to one of the protestors and said to me, "Do you see the book that guy is carrying?"

"Yeah, what of it?"

"That's a bit of Michigan history, right there in front of you," she said.

"What is it?"

"That's a copy of 'The Protocols of the Elders of Zion'," she said.

"Is that a Jewish book from Michigan?" I asked.

"Far from it. It's a vile anti-Semitic book written in Europe. Good old Henry Ford, the father of the modern automobile, from right here in Detroit, thought that the American public should be aware of the dangers of associating with Jews. Being the good Samaritan that he was, he had the book translated, printed, and distributed."

"That was nice of him," I said sarcastically.

We had gotten through most of the crowd when we heard someone shout, "There they are. Over there."

I looked back to see who 'they' were but instead saw a dozen men close in on us and grab both me and Dafna.

The grab was done most professionally. We did not stand a chance. It was almost as if they had rehearsed the grab.

Five guys held my arms and legs and one fellow had his arm tightly around my neck. Dafna was in the same boat.

The crowd was loudly encouraging the people holding us.

We both yelled and protested but no one was listening.

The mob cheered as they dragged us back up to the top of the steps in front of the building. Between us stood a thirty something young man with a red checkered *kafiyeh* wrapped around his neck and a three day beard on his face. He motioned for the protestors to be silent and began, "Today we strike a blow in the battle to achieve justice for the Palestinian people who are being oppressed by the Zionists."

The crowd loved it and roared their approval.

"These two Israeli Zionists tried to sneak into our community and spread their lies, but we know the truth. They will pay the price."

More cheers.

I could not believe this was happening in the middle of the day. In the middle of East Lansing. In the middle of the USA — land of the free.

We were just two blocks away from the police station and I was fairly sure that someone inside the building must have called the cops. If I could just stall this guy we would be all right. My head was pulled far back but I could still speak and I said, "You've got the wrong people. We're not Israeli. I live in Detroit and she lives here in East Lansing."

"Is your name not Simon Lincoln?" asked *kafiyeh man.* "And is this not Dafna Lachler?"

The guy had a slight Arab accent and pronounced the 'ch' sound in Lachler perfectly. How did this guy know our names? "Yes, that's our names but we are not Israeli."

The fellow turned to the crowd, "See how they lie." He held up a paper but I could not see what was written. "This is a warrant issued in the International Court of Justice in the Hague for the arrest and extradition of Simon Lincoln and his whore Dafna Lachler for war crimes committed against the Palestinian people during the Israel's unprovoked invasion of Gaza in the year 2014."

"What are you talking about? I have never been to Israel in my life," I exclaimed.

"More lies," screamed the man. "Here are their pictures. This is Captain Simon Lincoln of the Israel Defense Forces."

I looked around to see if anyone in the crowd might be able to help. The protestors were crowded around us at the base of the steps. There seemed to be ten or twelve real hotheads who were spurring on the rest of the crowd. They were not as enthusiastic as the ringleaders, but I could see that none were going to help us. No one from the Hillel building was venturing out the front door.

There were some curious passersby but they were keeping their distance by standing on the sidewalk across the street.

We were on our own.

In times of stress you sometimes notice the weirdest things. About one quarter of the people around us had their smart phones out and were recording the entire proceedings. No one was going to help, but they were going to document whatever happens, up the whazoo.

Dafna yelled out, "Are you crazy? You have the wrong people."

"How dare you talk to me like that. Close your mouth you stupid bitch," yelled *kafiyeh* man. Then he raised his hand, and with his open palm gave Dafna a resounding slap, that spun her head around.

It felt as if I was watching the whole thing in slow motion. I heard the sound of the slap and my blood began to boil. I tried to free myself but to no avail.

The crowd cheered.

"This man is a war criminal," he said pointing at me. "The police will be here soon and we will turn him over to them. But first you must hear what this man has done." The crowd quieted so as not to miss a word. "During the conflict, this man commanded an eight man squad. They entered the town of Beit Lahia in the Gaza Strip. Without provocation they broke into the UNRWA school — the United Nations School — and these 'heroes' captured an entire class of seventeen high school girls. He directed his men to rape each one of the girls. Those innocent young girls. Then when his men had their way, he ordered them to kill the entire class so that there would be no evidence of what they had done. And since they did not want to attract attention they did not shoot the girls. They slit their throats and left them to die. That is the criminal you see before you," he said pointing at me again. "He must be punished. Should he be allowed to walk free?" he screamed.

The crowd answered with a resounding, "No!!!!"

The fact that none of this was true was of no concern to any of the protestors. The aggressive dynamic of the crowd was reaching fever pitch.

I squirmed but I could not get free. I could only hope the police got here to rescue us before this crowd got out of hand.

"There is one more thing you do not know," shouted *kafiyeh* man. The noise abated slightly. "I come from Beit Lahia," he paused for effect. "That was my home. One of the girls that this man raped and murdered was my sister."

The crowd went crazy.

Where are the police?

I could hear the sirens approaching. It would not be long now.

Apparently he also heard the sirens and continued, "The police will soon arrive and when they do they will see what it means to be a true hero of Islam. To make Jihad — a holy war — against the Zionists." He extracted a ten inch hunting knife from his jacket. "I will take the life of this man's woman just like he took my sister's life." With his left hand he grabbed Dafna's hair and pulled. Her wig came off in his hand and that made him angry. He threw down the *Shaitel* and took a hold of her real hair, pulling her head back to expose her throat to the knife in his right hand. The crowd gasped and became silent. He stood poised and just looked around.

My heart skipped a beat. I thought Dafna was a goner. I tried to reason with him, "Why are you doing this? Put down the knife. If the police see you holding the knife like that they will have no choice but to shoot you."

"I know," he said with resolve. "I will show the world what it means to be a sacred martyr — a *shaheed* — one who receives seventy-two virgins as his reward in heaven."

So that was what he has planned. He wants to wait for the cops to arrive, then slit Dafna's throat knowing the cops would shoot him dead. Death by police. He gets to become a martyr and it makes the police look bad.

I heard the sirens at the end of the street. The cops were probably strategically deploying men before they closed in. That included snipers.

"Be silent," screamed *kafiyeh* man. "Remember this day so you may tell your grandchildren about it. Tell them how we fought for Islam," he ranted.

The crowd went silent.

I had less than thirty seconds to do something and I did not know what to do. I could see that there were two more fellows behind me ready with hunting knives. Perhaps they were the backup team if *kafiyeh* man did not succeed.

Time was running out.

I stopped struggling.

The men holding my arms relaxed slightly.

The crowd waited in silent expectation.

Then I took a deep breath and screamed at the top of my lungs the only thing I knew that would get their attention, "*Allah akbar*!!!!!"

Yelling out the most basic of Islamic chants was not in contradiction to anything I had learned in the *yeshiva*. It meant 'God is great'. Since I also believed in that and since we were talking about the same God, I had no problem surprising the aggressive rabble with that phrase.

It certainly had the desired effect.

Everyone looked around to see who had broken the silence with that most holy of prayers and that included the two goons holding my arms. As soon as I sensed that they were distracted I shot my right arm forward with all my strength. This broke the grip of the guy on my right and positioned my arm perfectly to bring my right elbow back rapidly into his nose. I heard the bones break as they pushed up towards his brain. The guy went down.

Without hesitating, I twisted my body to the left bringing my right fist across my body in a roundhouse to the chin of the guy on my left. His head snapped back and his eyes turned up. Normally I try not to hit anyone with my knuckles but I had no choice.

My hand hurt but I had two down.

I continued the motion of my body around to my left so that I was now facing the fellow with his arm around my neck. I pushed his body away from mine and rapidly brought my right knee up into his groin. It was not as good a hit as what Dafna had inflicted to the guy in the alley but it was adequate because I had a hundred pounds more inertia. The goon's testicles took a trip on the extra speedy up elevator directly into his skull. He released his grip and I head-butted him with all my strength. That was number three.

About four seconds had gone by since I invoked the name of God and all hell was breaking loose. Both guys with the knives were headed my way and *kafiyeh* man was screaming instructions to someone behind me. The first fellow with the blade was obviously not an experienced knife fighter. Instead of approaching slowly and using one of the two standard knife fighting techniques — those being slashing or stabbing — he lunged at me as if he was using a three foot sword.

That was a big mistake.

I should feel bad for any guy who made such an amateurish move but when I realized that he had intended to make me into a shish-kabob all my sympathy vanished.

I easily sidestepped the lunge and grabbed his outstretched arm with both my hands. I then brought his arm down rapidly onto my knee that I was bringing up. You could hear the bones break from a yard away.

Number four was out of commission and I now had a knife. Knife man number two was not much better than his friend. When he advanced with his knife extended I grabbed his arm and pulled. He had been moving forward and by pulling his hand I was able to accelerate his forward motion and spin him about. Once his back was to me I reached down and sliced my knife across the back of his knee. This cut the hamstring tendons and he went down unable to stand on that leg. He still had his knife but he was not going anywhere.

Many of the people in the crowd came to the logical conclusion that it was not a good idea to be in the vicinity of the brouhaha and they were taking the opportunity to skedaddle. Protestors were moving this way and that. I ducked low and hid from *kafiyeh* man who was yelling commands with his knife still poised against Dafna's neck. Why he decided to stick with his original script of waiting for the police to kill him I do not know. I am just thankful he did not try to improvise. I ducked behind a fellow with a large sign and pushed him towards *kafiyeh* man.

It would only take a slight motion of his hand to slice through Dafna's neck. If I was a split second too slow it could mean disaster. Somehow I had to incapacitate the use of his right hand.

As soon as I was parallel with *kafiyeh* man I pushed my human shield out of the way and with all my strength I stabbed my knife into his forearm. The blade hit bone and then continued right on through to the other side. He screamed in pain but most importantly he could not move any of the muscles in his right arm. His hand became lax and his knife clattered to the floor. I pulled Dafna away from his grasp and karate punched him with a straight right to the face.

I was angry and my execution was perfect. My sensei would have been proud. My ki — body energy — was focused about two feet behind his head. I was not sure if I had kept the force to below lethal level but I really would not be overly bothered if it was bit too strong and that his brain had exploded in his skull.

I followed the first hit with my left palm coming up directly to his chin and finally by my right palm breaking all his nasal bones. He was not dead and just stood there trying to decide if his ticket had been punched. Suddenly a really ticked off Dafna pushed me aside and kicked him in the crotch like she was going for a Super Bowl field goal.

It was decided. He went down.

Dafna was now jumping about on her left foot and complaining about her toe. I think I might have smiled at the humor of the situation.

She had not remembered about sturdy shoes.

I looked around quickly and could not see any more attackers.

A feeling of relief washed over me and everything started to become sort of a blur.

The police had finally arrived and were handcuffing anybody they could grab and were calling for medical support. The six heroes of Islam that I had laid out were scattered around the steps. All the rest of the protestors were crawling into the woodwork and making themselves scarce.

I don't know how it happened but at some point I began hugging Dafna and she was hugging me. I think we were holding each other up. We did not say anything, we just hugged. My mind was a blank but I do remember that it felt very comforting. In the back of my mind I knew that this was not the appropriate behavior for a *yeshiva bocher* with a woman that was not his wife but I felt that God wanted us to be hugging each other. It was the right thing to do. We stood like that until the initial pandemonium of the police raid abated ... about five minutes I think. Then she seemed to realize just what she was doing and broke away embarrassed for making such a display. She leaned closer and whispered emotionally, "I was so scared. So, so scared."

"Scared is good in this business. It keeps you from doing stupid things," I said. I retrieved my hat and Dafna's *shaitel*. The hat was not too bad, but her wig was a total mess and absolutely filthy from being trampled. She couldn't wear the thing so she just held it in her hand. Dafna looked so small and vulnerable and I knew she was on the verge of breaking, "Can I ask you something?"

"Anything," she answered meekly.

I looked at her sternly, "We are supposed to be 'kick *tuchis*' partners, right?" She nodded her head in agreement. "And I know you did all the work the last time with the mugger."

"You were kind of a wimp, you know," she said with a weak smile.

"But that was one guy. Big deal," I said dismissingly.

"That was a big deal for me," she said proudly.

"So, how come you just stood there today? I mean, there was just one guy holding a knife to your neck. You just did nothing and you left me to do all the hard work. That's not what I call a partnership. You better shape up." I said sarcastically.

For a moment she took me seriously but then she understood.

"I'll try not to be so lazy next time," she said with a wide smile.

"Now you're talking partner," I said with an equally broad smile.

We began to laugh.   The laughing got deeper and stronger.   Tears of happiness for being alive flowed down her cheeks.   Maybe mine as well.

Much better than tears of sorrow and death.

CHAPTER NINETEEN — White Chevrolet

"THE DEPUTY CHIEF AND the Mayor are already breathing down my neck," said Slatterly from across his desk. "What am I going to do with you two?"

I put the ice pack over the aching knuckles of my right hand and answered, "I am just an ordinary citizen visiting your fair city. What do you want from me?"

"Ordinary my foot. You two are a walking disaster area," he said in exasperation.

"None of this was our fault," said Dafna.

"That may be true, but we have never had such a crime wave in our city. We were a quiet little university town until you came along," said the cop.

It was now almost eight o'clock in the evening. We had made statements to the local police, the state police and the FBI. *Kafiyeh* man, a.k.a. Ali Muhammad Salim, had been on the federal watch list for his association with the Islamic State movement in the Middle East. All six fellows that I had taken out were still obtaining medical treatment and had yet to be officially booked into the system. The police were able to obtain twenty-two videos that documented all that had happened. Four videos had somehow been leaked and 'The Hillel House

Horror' was already being shown every fifteen minutes on the syndicated news shows.

In mock modesty I said, "I am only here to help the local public safety officials."

Slatterly said, "The Feds told us that Salim was boasting to anyone who would listen and that all the protestors were not locals. They came up here special from Dearborn."

That made sense, since Dearborn, a suburb of Detroit, had the highest Arab population of any city in the US. It was only logical that it would also be the home of any Arab extremists who supported radical causes.

"What do you mean that they came here 'special'? What were they trying to accomplish?" asked Dafna.

The cop answered as if he was stating the obvious, "To catch and kill you both."

"They were hired to kill us?" I asked.

"Nope," said Slatterly. "It was a freebee. They were recruited."

"By whom?" I asked.

"You know that paper Salim had in his hand?" asked the cop rhetorically. "It was an 'official alert' from Peace International telling the world about your 'crimes'."

"But it is a lie," I stated emphatically.

"You know that and I know that, and maybe Salim really knew it too. But for him that piece of paper was good enough," said Slatterly with a nod of his head. "They also received the counterfeit warrant from the Hague, and a clear description of what you both look like along with photographs."

"How did they get a picture of me?" I asked.

"Hacked it off your driver's license photo from the Secretary of State's DMV file," said Slatterly. "They even had a description of your black suit and fedora. Plus they were informed that you would be at the Hillel House at two o'clock. Who knew you would be there at two o'clock?"

"But, we didn't go there at two. We arrived at one," said Dafna.

"That's because they moved the meeting to one o'clock," I said.

"So who knew you were supposed to be there at two?" asked Slatterly.

I turned to Dafna, "Did your mother know?" She nodded in the affirmative and I turned back to Slatterly, "The whole world knew."

"Who fed them the false information about us?" asked Dafna

"Anonymous informant. Everything came to Salim via email. Three different messages, all from an East Lansing coffee shop that offers computer access."

"Did you check out the coffee shop," I asked.

Slatterly shook his head, "No leads there. No records and no video. We're still looking."

"So Mr. Salim, gets all this stuff, gathers a bunch of goons, fakes a protest, all in order to catch me?" I stated.

"Or it could be her," said Slatterly pointing at Dafna. "The email made a rather graphic suggestion that she should be killed."

"What about what Salim said, that his sister was raped and killed by the Israelis? Was that true?" I asked.

"It never happened. It was all bullshit. He was playing the crowd. The FBI says that Salim is an only child. But, considering that the report from Peace International was a fake and that there never was such an incident, what was one more lie," said Slatterly holding out his palms. "The Feds think that he was tipped off that he was about to go down for his terrorist activities and he thought suicide as a Islam martyr was better than an extended stay in Guantanamo. Catching you — Mr. Zionist criminal — and killing Dafna — would look good on his *shaheed* credentials. It was a perfect setup for Salim. He probably suspected that it all was a bunch of lies, but he did not care. He was looking for a good cause to die for. He made up the part about his sister to add dramatic effect. You know, crowd appeal."

"So someone wanted one or both of us dead," I said. The cop nodded his head in agreement. "Do you still think that none of this is related and that Klein was a suicide?"

"Look, I admit it could be, but we still haven't got a clue as to who it might be, how they did it, or why."

"We're working on it," said Dafna.

"And making a shambles of my city in the process," said the cop.

"Have you got anything on the white car?" I asked.

"Oh, do we ever," said Slatterly casting a glance at the ceiling. "Julie, tell them about the car."

Detective Dalton opened a small notebook and read off, "No one on that block owns a 2009 Chevy Malibu. As a matter of fact no one for a five block radius. Unfortunately there are over 7,000 of the 2009 models listed in a seventy five mile radius."

"But how many of them are white?" I asked.

"I'm getting to that," said Julie. "Only eight hundred are white. But then we hit a problem. Our auto expert looked at the video and he is convinced that although the front of the car is a Malibu, the rear-end is from an Impala model."

"So which is it," asked Dafna.

Slatterly said, "Both."

"How can it be both?" I asked.

"The Malibu and the Impala use a similar chassis," said Julie. "If the car was in a big wreck and the rear-end had to be fixed, someone could have spliced on an Impala rear end from another wreck."

"Is that possible?" asked Dafna.

Julie answered by spreading four pictures on the desk, "Take a look at these. The top two are the front ends of the Malibu and the Impala models. The bottom two the rear ends. Malibu on the right Impala on the left. See how the Malibu front has three horizontal bars and the Impala two. The Impala rear-end has rear lights that wrap around to the side, while the Malibu lights are only on the back. Distinctly different." She then placed two more pictures on the table. They were blurred and grainy and showed the front and rear sections of the white car from the surveillance video, "See ... front Malibu and rear Impala."

"And you say someone patched the rear-end of an Impala on a Malibu front?" I asked.

"Yup," said Julie with a nod of her head. "But it could be that someone put the Malibu front on an Impala. Our auto guys say it would take some interesting body work but it is definitely possible."

"Wouldn't who ever bought it notice this strange combination?" queried Dafna.

Slatterly looked at me and asked, "What do you say, would you notice?"

I had to admit that until just now I had not known how to differentiate between a 2009 Impala and Malibu so I would never have noticed. "No, I wouldn't."

Slatterly continued, "So, that almost doubles the number of cars we have to check because we don't know if the original car registration was for an Impala or a Malibu. Also, if it was in a wreck, then there is a good chance that white was not its listed color."

Dalton added, "So we have to look at all the Impalas and Malibus from the year 2009. And we don't even know if the car has a Michigan registration. It could have come from Ohio or anywhere. Add to that, the killer could have purchased the car for cash just to commit this crime. So, if he did not register the pink slip with the Secretary of State it will still be listed as belonging to the original owner."

"So you are saying there is no way you can find this car," I said.

Dalton shrugged her shoulders, "I am afraid not."

"That was our only real lead," I said in frustration. "Now we are up the creek without a paddle."

"There might be a way to find the car," ventured Dafna.

"How?" asked Dalton.

"Well, you said that the front is a Malibu and rear is an Impala. That's got to be pretty rare for a 2009 Chevy," stated Dafna.

"I would think so," said Slatterly. "There are maybe a dozen of those in the world."

"So just look for a 2009 Chevy with a Malibu front and an Impala back. Since it is so rare, if you find it, you have the suspect," said Dafna as if stating the obvious.

"There is no way to just ... look ... for a certain car," stated Slatterly. "It can't be done."

Dafna nodded her head rapidly and said, "Yes, it can."

I suddenly understood what Dafna was saying and I looked at her questioningly, "PlayStation?"

She turned to me and nodded her head, "PlayStation."

I pointed my thumb at Dafna and told Slatterly, "She can do it."

CHAPTER TWENTY — Slip Knot

IT WAS 10:30 IN the evening when we got to Dafna's house because we had to stop at the hospital to get her toe x-rayed. She broke it this time. They only had to tape her toes together, but for the next few days she was not going to be running around too much.

We were seated at her kitchen table and Mrs. Kalin was serving us the food that she had kept warm for us. Curried chicken on rice. It was delicious as always.

I hadn't had lunch or dinner and I could eat a horse.

Actually ... I couldn't.

Horse is not kosher.

I was already on my third helping and it was so good that I did not even mind that Dafna's mother had not stopped berating us since we entered the house.

She was really ticked off at both of us.

She was using her four questions over and over.

Most of her comments were about what big idiots we were. That we were to blame for all the problems that had plagued our investigation. She reminded us about the mugger, the car explosion, and now the attempted slaughter of Dafna.

As if we could forget.

It was almost midnight when we finally went down to the Vault. At least a couple of dozen people called but she did not pick up and all the calls went to voicemail.

"Are you up to this?" I asked Dafna.

"Do you mean can I do my computer wizardry after getting freaked out of my skull by almost getting killed again this afternoon and after only sleeping three hours in the past twenty-four? Is that what you mean?"

"Yeah," I said sheepishly.

"I can do it. Working the computers will keep my mind from delving too deep into what just happened. I'll be fine."

"How are you going to find the car?"

"If Slatterly gives me permission to enter the traffic surveillance systems for Shiawassee, Clinton, and Ingham counties that will make my life simpler. Once I get that, I will set my computers to recognize 2009 Chevys with a Malibu front and Impala back."

"White Chevys," I said correcting her.

"No, any color," she said correcting me. "If it was painted once it could have been painted again. So any color. What is not going to change is the Malibu-Impala combination."

"You are right. I did not think of that," I said with an acquiescent nod of my head.

Dafna made a mock bow as if accepting an accolade and continued, "Then I will go back to the night Rabbi Klein died and try to see where the car went after it left the vicinity of Rabbi Klein's house."

"You can do that? Go back over a month?" I asked.

"Used to be the systems worked with tapes, and there was no way to get that stuff. But now it's all digital and most cameras have a three month backup. So if I can get in, I can find it," she said.

"How many cameras are we talking about?" I inquired.

"I am not sure, but it is probably between three and four hundred."

"Are you kidding me? That's impossible," I exclaimed.

"Hey, if it was easy you would not need me," she said stoically.

"There is something else that was bothering me," I said.

"About the car?"

"No, about our discussion with Ms. Silverman at the Hillel house."

"What did she say?"

"It's what she didn't say."

"O.K., what didn't she say."

"She told us that her lawyers advised her not to mention anything about Rebbitzen Klein's accusations and her encounter. So, my questions is, what else is she not talking about?"

"What do you mean?"

"We assume that Rabbi Klein is a good guy. Doing volunteer work in helping students that had emotional problems."

"Suicidal problems," she corrected.

"Exactly," I said with a nod of my head. "What if he was not always successful?"

"What do you mean 'not successful'? That he did not show up for a meeting with a student" she asked.

"No, what if he was not successful in preventing a suicide?"

"That could happen."

"Sure it could. And what would the families of the person that killed themselves think of Rabbi Klein?"

"That he was not successful. That's obvious."

"Not so obvious," I corrected. "It is just possible that they could think that he or the Hillel House are responsible."

"Wow, you're right. Do you think that's who killed Rabbi Klein?"

"I have no idea, but we need to check out that possibility."

"Should we contact Ms. Silverman and ask her?"

"Waste of time."

"Why do you say that?"

"Because they did not mention it to Frank DeAngelo, because if they did he would have looked into it."

"So how can we know which of the students that committed suicide here at the university were counseled by Rabbi Klein?" she asked.

"First of all, we don't want a list of the kids that killed themselves. We just want the ones that think Hillel House or Rabbi Klein were responsible."

"Same problem."

"Not exactly," I explained. "Years ago, if you thought that someone did something bad to you, you would settle it by some sort of an altercation. Physical or verbal. We don't do that anymore."

"What do we do now?"

"We take them to court and sue the pants off the guy that hurts you."

"I see what you mean. We don't need a list of the suicide victims we need the list of the people that sued Hillel House or Rabbi Klein."

"I don't want to know about a suit filed for falling in the hall of the Hillel House. I want to see the ones for failing to prevent a suicide."

Dafna turned to her keyboard and began typing, "Give me a second."

Screens came up and disappeared. Dafna noted something that flashed for a moment on the screen and said, "Tricky, tricky." Then she typed some more commands. After five minutes she pointed to an item that appeared on a Google search. "This could be it."

The screen showed a report from the New York Post from four years earlier. Marcia Weinstein, the only child of George and Alice Weinstein, of New York City, had been a student at Michigan State. She dropped out of school, returned to New York and committed suicide. Six months after her death her despondent father, George, took an overdose of sleeping pills and ended his life. Alice Weinstein blamed both deaths on the improper handling of her daughter's problem by the Hillel House who had referred her daughter for counseling with Rabbi Klein, who was not a professional psychotherapist. Because she was a resident of New York State, she sued the Hillel House Foundation, which was based in New York, for two million dollars. Mrs. Weinstein lost the case at trial and then on appeal and was required to pay the hefty court costs.

"Where is dear old Alice now? She could still be ... angry with Hillel House and Rabbi Klein."

I wanted to say 'pissed off', but I knew that Dafna would not approve.

"Let's see," she said, hitting some more keys.

I watched the screen but everything changed so quickly I had no idea what I was seeing, "Is she still living in New York?"

She turned from the monitor and said with a quizzical look on her face, "She does not seem to be anywhere."

"Unless she is dead, she has got to be somewhere."

"Well, she never paid the court costs, so her house was grabbed by the courts. She has not paid income tax. Has no address or bank accounts in the USA. She just vanished."

"Mrs. Weinstein, could be our murderer. Can you locate a picture of her. For all I know, she could be someone affiliated with the *kollel*."

Dafna said, "If she killed Rabbi Klein ... then I can see why she made it look like a suicide."

"It is very possible that she has nothing to do with the case but she is our first real suspect."

"So, you admit that *Rebbitzen* Klein did not do it," she said with satisfaction.

"I did not say that," I corrected. "Just, try to find Alice Weinstein."

"I'll see what I can do," she said.

"Don't forget, you also have to find the car."

"How could I forget? Just go back to your hotel so I can work. Get a couple of hours of sleep for me as well.

∞

I returned to the hotel and there was a message waiting on my room phone. Rabbi Kalmonowitz wanted me to call him no matter what time I got back.

I placed my dirty hat on the dresser and brushed off my jacket as best I could before hanging it in the closet. It needed to be sent to the dry cleaners but that would have to wait. My shirt had blood speckles all over the front — not mine — and it would have to go in the pile of dirty laundry. First I needed to loosen my tie. I really am terrible at tying a Windsor. I usually do not get the two ends to come out where they should. So I just loosened the loop around my neck and took off the tie, leaving the knot intact.

With the tie in my hand I sat down on the bed and called Rabbi Kalmonowitz. He answered his phone on the third ring, "Good morning *Reb* Shimon. Are you well?"

I had no idea how the rabbi knew it was me, "I'm fine rabbi. My right hand is a little sore but otherwise fine."

"I saw how you hit that fellow," said the rabbi. "*Yosher koach* — blessing of praise, meaning literally 'may your strength increase'."

How had Rabbi Kalmonowitz seen the Hillel House incident, he did not watch TV? "It was nothing, *Rebbi*," I said belittling what I had done.

"It was not nothing," he said in praise. "I saw it on Ephraim's telephone screen — amazing what the phones can do nowadays. Not many people could have done what you did. You are a *gibor* — hero — and what you did is a real *kiddush HaShem* — you brought praise to God."

Wow, that was something coming from Rabbi Kalmonowitz, "Thank you, *Rebbi*."

"Now, tell me please how you have progressed," said the rabbi politely.

I started with the report from the pathologist and continued with what we had learned at the Hillel House. I also told him all the revelations concerning the protestors and how we had been made the targets of the attack by some unknown person who had fed the false information to Salim. I ended with the search for the Malibu/Impala 2009 Chevy and our new suspect, Mrs. Weinstein.

Rabbi Kalmonowitz remained silent for a moment and then said, "You know that this is all related to *Rav* Avraham's death, don't you?"

"Yeah, I am certain you are right."

"It also means that you must be getting close to finding the killer," stated the rabbi.

"I hope so," I said.

"I know so," said the rabbi with determination. "The killer made a mistake. He left evidence of how he did it and who he is."

I sensed that Rabbi Kalmonowitz knew something. I wish he would share it with me. "We're trying."

"Try harder. It is right in front of you."

"What is?"

"The evidence," he said as if stating the obvious. "And *Reb* Shimon, if they tried to kill you, they are getting desperate. Be careful and take extra special care of *Rebbitzen* Lachler, she is precious. Good night and thank you for all you have done."

He hung up.

Rebbitzen Lachler! So her husband had actually been a rabbi. I thought of Dafna and was amazed at her abilities. Not just with the computer. She was so brave and so smart. I had never met a woman quite like her. I enjoyed her company and looked forward to seeing her tomorrow.

Uh oh. Where is this leading? Don't go reading things into that hug. That was purely emergency psychological therapy. No emotional context at all.

For her.

But what about me?

Take it easy. It will all be over soon. She will forget you and you will forget her.

No, I won't, but it will be a fond memory.

What did Rabbi Kalmonowitz mean when he said it was right in front of me?

I was still holding the tie in my hand sliding the tail through the knot, when I realized that it was very similar to the noose that had been tied around the neck of Rabbi Klein. I looked at the slip knot and had a revelation. It was right there in front of me. I took a quick look at the file and ran through the crime scene pictures that I had on my phone and I was sure that I was right.

I now had proof that Rabbi Avraham Klein had been murdered.

CHAPTER TWENTY ONE — Who Done It

SHAINDEL KALIN OUTDID HERSELF the next morning. Spicy hash browns combined with green onion scrambled eggs and fresh vegetable salad. I am not a big salad eater but the garlic dressing was scrumptious.

As I chewed my way to bliss I once again commended myself on my decision to dump all the provisions that I had brought up from Detroit. They were four days old and even when they were fresh they could not compare with this food. I was trying very hard not to wolf down my breakfast. Dafna's daughters barely touched their own plates and just giggled every time I took a bite.

They don't know how good their grandma cooks. When they get older they are in for a big surprise.

Dafna came limping up from the Vault wearing the same clothes that she had worn the day before. A *tichel* covered her hair instead of her dirty *shaitel*. She plopped down in a chair and said, "Coffee, now."

Disheveled, exhausted, and wearing no makeup, it was really good to see her.

I definitely have a problem.

"Good Morning," I said cheerfully.

She held up a palm like a traffic cop, "Not yet, coffee first."

Mrs. Kalin brought her a cup and she took a sip, "Ahhh."

I waited a moment and tried to make conversation, "I am so enjoying your mother's cooking. It is terrific. You should ask her to give you lessons. It couldn't hurt," I added jokingly.

Dafna made a tepid smile and said, "I will surely ask her, thanks for the advice."

Shaindel started laughing but when she saw that I did not know what was funny she said "You're kidding me. You really don't know?"

"Don't know what?" I queried.

Mrs. Kalin pointed at her daughter and said, "She usually tells everyone as soon as they come in the door."

"Mom, it's not important," said Dafna with a tired shake of her head.

"It sure is important," said the older woman. "When I came here two years ago, after David, *alav hashalom*, passed away. I was supposed to help cook. The problem was I really did not know how. My husband never complained, he was a generous soul. My meals were pathetic. More than pathetic, they were a disaster."

"They were not that bad," said Dafna encouragingly.

Shaindel turned to Dafna's daughters, "Girls, how was my cooking back then?"

Susie pinched her nose indicating that the meals were terrible and Aliza gave a thumbs down, shook her head and said with a grimace, "Not good at all."

"You just needed a little help," said Dafna.

"And I got it. Someone taught me how to cook. Do you know who that someone was?"

"I haven't got the foggiest," I answered.

"Mom!" exclaimed Dafna.

She pointed at Dafna with both open palms, "My daughter. She took me in hand and taught me the difference between frying and sautéing. Between mixing and folding and all the other crazy cooking skills that I had never acquired. Then she wrote down all her recipes and stood at my side as I learned to prepare them. Everything I have made in the last few days are Dafna's recipes."

Whammy! Not only was she pretty, smart and a genius at the computer, she could cook. "You know how to cook?"

"Why are you so surprised," asked Dafna slightly offended.

"Because I haven't seen you cook a single thing since I have been here," I said in my defense.

"Duh ... we have been kind of busy these last few days," said Dafna.

The work on the computer, the mugger, the grenade, and the Jihad attack flashed through my mind. She was right. We had been busy.

"Does that mean after we solve this case you'll cook me something?" I ventured.

"Okay, here's the deal. Solve the case and I'll cook you dinner," she challenged.

Was I reading something into her remark? Could it be that she enjoyed my company as much as I did hers? "Let's get to work," I said eagerly.

∞

Dafna walked with her shoulders slumped from lack of sleep. We went into the Vault. She put her refilled coffee cup on the desk and asked me, "Did you accomplish anything since I saw you last?"

"I spoke with Rabbi Kalmonowitz last night and he told me that the proof that Rabbi Klein was murdered was right before my eyes."

"And was it?" she asked.

"Actually, it was," I said simply.

She said, "With Rabbi Kalmonowitz, you can take it to the bank."

I then explained the discovery that I had made with my neck tie.

Dafna nodded her head in approval, "Pretty sharp. What did the police have to say about that?"

"Nothing yet. I wanted to run it past you before I showed it to Slatterly."

"This is very important," said Dafna. "The cops have been humoring us. They are not really convinced that this was a murder. Once you show them what you discovered they will have no choice but to reopen the entire investigation. Nice work."

Those words of praise were especially nice coming from Dafna. I realized that I wanted her to appreciate me. No, I wanted her to like me. Maybe more.

I'm in serious trouble here.

I tried to change the subject. "And what did you accomplish during your night without sleep.

She leaned back in her chair and unfolded a sheet of paper. This is a picture of Alice Weinstein. It's ten years old, and was taken from the catalog of the sporting goods company she worked for. She was a salesperson. I still have no idea where she could be."

The picture was a bit grainy but was still a good head shot. Her hair would probably be greyer, or perhaps it was dyed, but either way I could not identify her. It was not someone I had encountered during the investigation.

That was a relief.

"I'll get the picture to Slatterly and see what they can do about locating her. What about the car?

She pointed at a map on the computer screen, "That's where your car is."

I was confused. My car was in little pieces being studied for bomb residues, "My car is in the State Police Lab."

"Not, your car. The white Chevy. I have not discovered where the car went after the rabbi died but I do know that on the following night the car left the city and went into this four square mile area of Shiawassee County," she said pointing to the map showing on the screen.

"You're sure it is there?" I asked.

"All I know right now, is that it went into that area and did not come out on that night. I'm going through all the cameras in that area to see when and if it came out. I'm about half way through and it looks like it is still there."

"Where exactly?" I wanted to know.

"Can't pin it down," she said in frustration. "Could be in a garage, parked on the road, out in the open. Your guess is as good as mine. I can only say it did not pass any of the cameras on the surrounding roads. Of course, if the killer took dirt roads or went off-road completely, that's a different story, but I'm 99% sure this is where it is."

"I'll inform the police, but we still don't know for sure that this car had anything to do with the killing," I said.

"It does prove one thing," said Dafna.

"What?" I asked.

"*Rebbitzen* Klein did not murder her husband," she said with confidence.

"How are you so sure?"

"Because, if the white Chevy is the vehicle that brought the killer to the Klein house, and if we assume that Alice Weinstein or whoever is the killer was working alone ... Do you agree with me so far?" asked Dafna looking at me.

"Yeah, I do."

"Then, whoever drove it the next night is the murderer. Because the Chevy left the city at one o'clock in the morning on the night after the rabbi's funeral in Detroit. Devorah got back to the house at 8:00 in the evening and she did not leave the house again for the seven days of the *shiva* — official mourning period."

"She could have snuck out," I suggested.

"No she couldn't," said Dafna. "For the entire *shiva* one of the women in the community was with her at all times. *Rebbitzen* Lipsky slept with her that night. Sneaking out on the very night your husband was buried would not go unnoticed. Also there is no record in the alarm company files that anyone left or entered the house once the alarm was set."

I was not going to ask her how she knew what the alarm company's records showed.

"That whole alarm business is what makes this case so strange. There must be a way to get into that house without triggering the alarm, otherwise how did the killer get in ... and out?

"You are absolutely right. Aliens could have dropped the murderer into the house from their flying saucer," suggested Dafna sarcastically.

"I get your point," I said. "So we are agreed, that it was not the *rebbitzen*."

"It just can't be her," said Dafna.

"Can't be her or you don't want it to be her?"

"Both."

Rebbitzen Klein was a strange woman and strange always sent up a red flag on my suspect radar. Still she had good alibis for the critical times in this case and there was no clear evidence that showed she was involved. I wanted Dafna's help in sorting out the facts, "She could have been the one who erased the files on the computer."

"Could have been the rabbi or someone else," she said.

"Who else?" I asked.

"I could have done it," said Dafna simply.

"Why would you do that?" I asked.

"I did not say I did it. But I or maybe a few hundred other hackers in this state could have done it."

"So, tell me again why it could not be her," I said.

Dafna began ticking things off on her fingers, "First, she was not home. The tapes in the theater, her phone GPS confirm this."

"Her phone GPS just means her phone did not leave the theater. She could have stashed it somewhere," I said.

Dafna looked at me questioningly, "Can I continue." I nodded in the affirmative. "Second, if she left the theater to sneak back to the house she would need some sort of transportation since the tapes show that her car never left the lot. No cabs came to the theater or any of the nearby lots and the white car was not parked anywhere near the theater before the murder. Third, if she came home how did she get past the alarm?"

I interjected, "Someone was able to get past the alarm. It could have been her."

"It could have been, but also could have been Alice Weinstein or my Grandma Zeesa. But she has an alibi better than *Rebbitzen* Klein ... she's dead," said Dafna.

"OK, I have just got to get it clear in my head that just because there must be a way around the alarm system, it does not mean that Devorah Klein was the one that killed her husband," I stated. "Continue."

Dafna took off where she had left off, "Fourth, She is not strong enough to choke her husband and certainly could not hoist him up so as to hang him from the water pipe. And if he was killed elsewhere in the house she did not have the strength to *shlep* him down to the basement. Fifth, assuming she got out of the house and got back to the white car, where did she leave it until it was driven out of the city the next day? It had to be near the theater otherwise she would not have had enough time. So if the car was near the theater where was it? That was over an entire day. None of the businesses in the area are open twenty four hours."

"Like a 24 hour superstore," I said.

"Exactly," she said with a nod of her head. "So, that means their lots are empty at night and the white Chevy would stand out." She pointed at her screen, "No Chevy on the tapes,"

"So, all we have so far, is that the rabbi was murdered and it could not have been the *rebbitzen*," I said.

"We're almost back where we started," said Dafna.

"I am still bothered by her threatening the Hillel House director," I said. "We both know the r*ebbitzen* is a little weird, but I think this goes over the line. If she didn't have that iron clad alibi, my gut feeling is that I should be honing in on her."

"The murderer could be Alice Weinstein or could be one of the students that he had counseled at the Hillel House. You know a little flirting, more flirting, things go bad, they go a little crazy," offered Dafna.

"You read too many mystery novels. There are two reasons I don't like that choice," I said. "Firstly, no opportunity. How could they get into his home and cover up everything they did? This was obviously planned in advance. And if the white car is part of this, it had to be well in advance. It is too complex for a crazy student to plan and execute. Second, Frank DeAngelo's report. I know him, his investigations were always exhaustive and complete. If he says there was no inappropriate behavior at the Hillel House then it's a 99% bet the rabbi did not have any extracurricular activities going on at the campus."

"It still could be Alice Weinstein or some nut job that we don't know."

"It could be the man in the moon and we'll never find him, but if you stick with motive and opportunity, you usually get your man." As an afterthought I added, "or woman."

"Would you stop already. The *rebbitzen* had no motive," said Dafna. "It could not have been for money. There was no insurance and she has all the money in the family. They were a terrific couple right to the end. There was no sign of difficulties between them."

"What does that prove? If she is the one who murdered the rabbi then she is lying now. And that means that she most likely has not been telling us the truth about them being a great couple."

"But why would Rabbi Klein behave like they were a great couple if they were not?" asked Dafna.

"He behaved that way because what good would it do not to? It would only embarrass them both, so he played along. We still don't know why he was seeking psychiatric help. It could have been that there was a problem in the marriage because of him. But that doesn't make sense, since that would make me think more that it was suicide."

Dafna said, "Regarding his psychiatric problems, I got through to Dr. Felix this morning ... the doctor whose charges were wiped from the disk. I asked him to give me information regarding Rabbi Klein's visits. He refused, saying it fell under the doctor-patient confidentiality rule. I told him what you said, that since the rabbi was dead the rule did not apply. He continued to insist that he could not give me any information, but would gladly comply if we got a court order."

"So, what are we going to do?" I asked.

"I am going to wait for him to connect to his external disk so I can see his files," she said.

"We could just ask the *rebbitzen* directly. It would save us a great deal of time," I said.

"Oh no, we can't," said Dafna sternly. "The visits to the doctor could be about something completely private that has nothing to do with this case. She would be mortified."

"When will we know for sure that the Chevy is still in your four square miles of Shiawassee county?"

"This afternoon," she answered. "When are you going to the police?"

"As soon as I leave here. I already told Slatterly I was coming over."

"You know the police are not going to like this?"

"Yeah, I know," I admitted.

"Nobody likes it when you point out that they made a mistake. So I can imagine cops are no different. They are going to be very angry when you show them that this was definitely not a suicide."

"Up until now, they have been humoring me with their investigation," I said. "None of them have been breaking out in a sweat in their efforts to look for the murderer or the car. Now they will have no choice."

Mrs. Kalin screamed from the top of the stairs, "Dafna, *Rebbitzen* Klein is here."

"That's strange," said Dafna.

"What's strange?"

"Devorah always ... I mean always ... calls and makes appointments before going to someone's home. She never just drops in."

"She is here now," I said stating the obvious. "Let's go say hello."

CHAPTER TWENTY TWO — Murder

THE *REBBITZEN* WAS SEATED on a kitchen chair in her normal position, half a *tuchis* on and half a *tuchis* off the chair. She was sipping a cup of tea when we entered, but stood when she saw us and approached Dafna with concern on her face.

I suppose a normal woman would have hugged Dafna, but of course Devorah Klein did not do hugs.

"Dafnaleh, oh Dafnaleh. You have no idea how worried I was for you," said the *rebbitzen* emotionally. "That man held you with a knife .... Oh my God. You are so brave."

That's interesting. How did she know that? The Kleins, like other Ultra-Orthodox Jews did not have a TV. Then I realized she could watch the news on her computer.

"There really was not much bravery involved," said Dafna. "He was holding me by my hair and had a knife to my throat. I just stood there and tried not to move."

"I would have died on the spot," said *Rebbitzen* Klein.

"Please sit down," said Dafna.

We all found seats while Shaindel fixed us up with coffee.

Dafna took a sip from her cup and asked the *rebbitzen*, "Is there something you need? You usually do not come without calling first."

"I know, but I called a dozen times and no one answered," said Devorah in explanation.

"That's true," said Dafna. "We have been busy."

"I am just beside myself with worry," she said. "After all, everything that happened to you is my fault."

That got my attention, "How so?"

"You are both investigating the death of my late husband," she said looking from me to Dafna. "You are doing this for his memory and my peace of mind. I feel responsible. If either of you were hurt I don't know what I would do."

"The risks come with the job," I said.

Then Dafna proudly repeated after me, "The risks come with the job."

"I just wish to thank you both. It means so much to me," she said emotionally.

Once again I saw that little flutter in her eyes. She was hiding something. I just did not know what it could be.

"We are happy to do it," said Dafna.

There was an awkward silence and then the *rebbitzen* asked, "Was the attack of the Arabs related to my husband's death?"

"Apparently so," responded Dafna. "They wanted to stop Mr. Lincoln from continuing his investigation."

The *Rebbitzen* looked at me and then said with a sigh of relief "*Baruch HaShem*, they were not successful."

Dafna then told Devorah how someone had used the internet to set us up with the Dearborn rabble.

"Unbelievable," said Devorah, shaking her head from side to side to accentuate her disbelief. Then, as if it was an afterthought, "Have you made any progress in my husband's death?"

I know that Dafna is convinced that the *Rebbitzen* is in the clear but I did not like her sharing any more information with *Rebbitzin* Klein, but there was little I could do to stop her short of shouting out, 'I think you may have killed the rabbi'.

"Actually, yes," said Dafna. She then explained to the *rebbitzen* my revelation with my neck tie.

The *rebbitzen* looked at me and said, "How clever of you."

I shrugged and said, "That's why they pay me the big bucks."

Devorah looked confused, "Someone paid you 'big bucks'?"

"It's just an expression," explained Dafna.

The lady had absolutely no sense of humor.

Devorah stated, "So that means that there is no doubt that it was not a suicide."

"Absolutely," stated Dafna confidently.

"So who do the police suspect?" she asked. "They must have some suspects."

"Actually, they don't," I said. I did not want to mention Alice Weinstein until we had more information. "They have not as yet seen my proof that it was a homicide, but I will be going over there in a few minutes. We're also still trying to figure out how the murderer got past your security system."

"I never thought of that," said the *rebbitzen* with a vexed expression.

Yes, she did.

There had been a little eye flutter.

"Right now we are looking for a car that we think was the vehicle that the murderer used," said Dafna.

"You found the murderer's car?" asked *Rebbitzen* Klein with interest.

"We have not found it. We are looking for it. A white Chevy," said Dafna.

"And when you find that car, how will it help your investigation?" she asked.

"That depends on where we find it and what we find in it," I said. "Most criminals are careless and they make mistakes. By studying the mistakes we find the criminals. We are very hopeful."

"*Baruch HaShem*, for stupid criminals," said the *rebbitzen*. "I see you have your work cut out for you. If there is anything I can do to help, please just ask."

Now was my opportunity to ask her about the visits to the psychologist. "There is something," I said with my most beguiling smile. "We were wondering ...". I saw Dafna shaking her head ever so slightly. She had read my

intentions and was asking me not to grill the *rebbitzen*. "
... could you think of us in your prayers. Wish for our
success."

Devorah smiled broadly and that made her nose dip
sharply, "Believe me. You are in my prayers all the time."

What did that mean?

∞

"What was so important that you had me call Dalton from
an active investigation?" asked Slatterly, putting his feet
up on his desk.

Julie Dalton pulled up a chair and looked at me
inquisitively.

I surveyed them both and began, "You remember when
you told me about how the rabbi died that he threw the
rope over the water pipe, tied it off and then put the
noose over his head and stepped off the chair. That is
also the way Detective Dalton wrote it up in her notes."

"Yeah, so what?"

"Think about it for a second," I said. "Why did you say it
in that order? Why couldn't he have put the noose over
his head and then throw the rope over the water pipe
and tie it off?"

Julie answered, "Because the rope was tied to a post that
was out of his reach once he was standing on the chair."

"Exactly, so Rabbi Klein was standing on the chair when
he put the noose around his neck," I said.

"Of course," said Slatterly. "That's the only way he could
have done it."

"Now look at these pictures," I said. I put down a half dozen pictures showing the rabbi's body hanging from the rope. "What do you see?"

"Stop playing games," said Slatterly angrily. "We see the body but what is it you want us to see? Obviously it is something we missed ... so explain."

"Look at the different shots taken from different angles," I said pointing to the pictures. "How far below the seat of the chair are the victim's ankles."

Dalton looked carefully at a few of the shots and said, "About three or four inches."

"Yeah, that's about right," agreed Slatterly.

"Now look at his neck," I instructed.

"I see the rope squeezing the hell out of his neck," said the sergeant.

"Correct again," I agreed. "The pathologist estimates that the rabbi's neck circumference in life was seventeen inches or about a six inch diameter. When the rabbi stepped off the chair and he was hanging on the rope, the circumference went down to twelve inches or a four inch diameter. This crushed his windpipe and cut off the blood flow to the brain."

"Are you giving us a lesson in pathology?" asked Slatterly.

"Just give me a second," I insisted. "So, if he stepped off the chair with the noose around his neck he would wind up about four inches below the chair."

Slatterly said testily, "That's exactly what we see in the pictures."

"Yes," I agreed. "But in order to get the rope over his head the rabbi would have had to open up the noose to about thirty inches circumference or a ten inch diameter."

"Of course," said Slatterly impatiently. "That's how you put on a noose."

"Exactly, but to get that slack you have to slide the noose back up on the rope," I said.

"So what?" asked Slatterly angrily.

"Don't you see?" I asked.

"Oh yeah," said Dalton in surprise. "How did I miss that?"

"Miss what," asked a confused Slatterly.

"He's too high," said Dalton.

"Who is too high?" asked Slatterly.

I just sat back and let Julie explain things to Jumpin' Jack.

"The rabbi is," said Julie. "There is no way he could have put the loosened noose over his head if he was standing on the chair. It would have been six or eight inches too high for him to reach it. After all he couldn't jump up and push his head through. And if it had been low enough for him to get the noose over his head he should have been six or eight inches lower than he is in these pictures."

Jumpin' Jack picked up the pictures and after studying them carefully threw them down angrily and said, "Holy crap, you are right. I did not really buy your water bottle business and the missing urine thing before, but all that has changed. This is a homicide."

For the next two hours I worked with Julie Dalton going over the material Dafna and I had gone through and all the information in the case file from the new murder perspective. I told them how Dafna had isolated the white Malibu/Impala Chevy in an area of Shiawassee County and Slatterly put out an alert to the county sheriff.

The police officially opened a homicide investigation of the Rabbi Klein case and Slatterly pulled in two more detectives to work on the file. I gave them the picture of Alice Weinstein and all the information related to the suit against Hillel House and Rabbi Klein. His people would investigate.

He also asked me not to investigate the people closest to the Rabbi because he wanted his detectives to question them first. They were through with me for now and my plans for talking to some of the suspects were put on hold. I decided this was a good time to make a visit to Eagle Security, the company that monitored the Klein house. Maybe they could tell me how someone could bypass the system.

Eagle was located about a half mile from Celebration! Cinema in south Lansing, the huge movie complex that *Rebbitzen* Klein had visited on the night her husband was killed. Since I was in the area, I decided to swing down Edgewood Boulevard to see the theater complex for myself. Just as described, the giant freestanding complex was far back from the main road and surrounded on three sides by parking lots. The south side had a much smaller lot because it backed up to the I-96 freeway. There were a few chain restaurants between the complex and Edgewood Boulevard and they too were surrounded by parking lots. Even the Edgewood Towne Center, a large strip mall to the east of the theaters was just another island in a sea of parking lots. There were no

alleys, no indoor garages and no hiding places for the
white Chevy.

If it was Alice Weinstein ... where could she be hiding. I
could not come up with a thing. It was hard to make my
mind switch to where I did not suspect the *Rebbitzen*.

My gut plays tricks on me.

I had to work on that.

I drove down the road slowly looking at the buildings in
the distance when I suddenly saw something we had not
noticed before. For some reason it just didn't show on
any of the surveillance videos. Just off the Boulevard on
American Road, was the WILX TV station. It had a small
broadcast tower and an even smaller building/studio.
The station had a small ten space parking lot.

This place was unique.

It was open 24 hours and it was very likely that no one
would notice if a white Chevy just happened to be parked
there overnight.

There I go again.

Rebbitzen Klein had an alibi and she could not have done
it.

Stop that.

I drove over to Eagle and met with their head engineer,
Mike Sangwin. When we sat down, he asked me to turn
off my cell phone while in the engineering section
because it interfered with some of their monitoring
equipment. Then we went to a conference room and he
was more than happy to pull all the records on the Klein
house and show me the alarm registry for the dates in

question. He spread all the data in front of us on a table and went through each of the documents thoroughly. To my specific question concerning a bypass switch for any of the doors, he showed me the circuit diagrams and specs for the system, indicating that there were no bypass switches. The place was inspected every two years to check the integrity of the system and the last inspection was two months before the rabbi died. If there had been such a switch on any of the doors or windows the inspector would have indicated it on the report.

So, I still had no idea how the murderer had gotten past the security system.

As I was leaving Eagle Security I switched my phone back on and noticed that one half hour earlier I had received a text message from Dafna.

WHITE CHEVY SPOTTED AT 9369 W BRITTON RD, JUST EAST OF WOODBURY RD IN LAINGSBURG, SHIAWASSEE, MICHIGAN

This was great news. The Shiawassee County Sheriff's Department deserves a commendation.

But why did I get the message from Dafna and not the police and why didn't she just call me?

I called Dafna's phone but it went straight to her voice mail.

Strange.

I was on the southwest side of the Greater Lansing area and the address given in the text message was to the northeast, in a rural area I had never visited. I keyed the address into the navigation system on my smartphone. Not as fancy as the GPS I had in my own car before it was blown to smithereens, but it would get me to my destination. The system said it would take twenty seven minutes and it usually knew what it was talking about.

This could be the break we were looking for.

With great optimism I hit the starter and the little red Hyundai coughed and sputtered until the motor caught and then it courageously conveyed me towards the next step in the investigation.

CHAPTER TWENTY THREE — Small Caliber

JUST THREE MILES NORTH of the East Lansing city limits, the area was mostly gentrified rural. Well back from the black top roads, recently constructed large multi-storied homes sat cradled in expansive manicured lawns. The new owners had apparently purchased working, or non working farms, and built their new homesteads in place of the old. The distance between the houses ranged from a hundred yards up to a quarter mile. The plots these homes sat on ranged from a couple of acres to over thirty or forty. The space between the brilliant green lawns was occupied by fallow fields, meadows, and pastures. Here and there you could see the remains of a crop of corn or where hay had been harvested in the past. Some of the 'homesteads' had barns and stables, for the well groomed pleasure horses that nibbled grass in nearby meadows.

Every half mile or so, you would be surprised by an actual working farm. These were easily identified by the barns and outbuildings that were obviously in use and the farm equipment parked around the buildings. The fields that surrounded these farms were either plowed, planted or getting ready for harvest. They also did not have manicured lawns.

The land was like most of Michigan, undulating flat with small creeks and streams that flowed towards the multiple lakes that dotted the surrounding countryside. The trees that lined the roads were interrupted only by farm tracks leading up into a field or the entrance roads to the 'homesteads'.

My navigation system announced that I had reached my destination and at first I thought it had made a mistake. The nearest buildings were at least a quarter of a mile away. But then I noticed that about one hundred yards from the road there was a small depression in the land surrounded by a copse of trees and I caught a glimpse of the roof of some sort of building. There was a small break in the trees and I saw a dirt track that headed in the general direction of the depression. The track was overgrown with weeds but vehicles had traveled on the road in the not too distant past.

I wondered why I had not spotted any police vehicles and debated whether I should investigate on my own or wait for the cops.

Considering that the text message had come through almost an hour before, I figured most likely they had already been there and gone.

A false lead.

That was probably it.

If I was already here I might as well have a look.

The dirt track swung wide around the distant trees and then down a small incline to wind up in the shade of the trees. Running in the bottom of the depression was a small stream and next to it, on a small knoll, was an old stone foundation. The house that had been sitting on this foundation was long gone and three inch saplings and tall weeds were sprouting between the rocks. Fifty yards from where the house had been was a barn-like structure. It was oblong in shape with a large double door on the narrow side facing the foundation. I estimated its size as about forty five feet on the long side and thirty on the short. It looked as if it had last been painted around the time of the Great Depression and the Michigan winters had turned most of the boards a dull grey in color. For all its age, the walls and roofline were still ruler straight. One of the original settlers in the area had built a commendably sturdy barn and in the last decade some recent settler had applied new shingles.

The track went right up to the large doors of the barn.

I got out of my car and cautiously walked all around the building keeping a distance of at least ten yards between myself and the structure.

Nothing unusual.

Except for the front of the building which was windowless, there were two filthy windows on each side. Looking through a dirty pane of glass it was not hard to see the white 2009 Chevy Malibu/Impala sitting in the middle of the barn.

This was not a false lead.

Why weren't the police here with the whole CSI team?

I tried the large front door and the right side swung out on well-oiled hinges. The barn was musty and dark with the only illumination coming from the light that forced its way through the grime coating the windows. I allowed my eyes to get accustomed to dim light and noticed that there was a work bench that ran the length of the right side and cupboards and shelves on the left. The back wall had a collection of old machinery and just plain junk.

I looked into the car and saw that there was a pile of things laying on the back seat. The CSI teams would have to study this stuff so I did not want to open the door or touch anything but it was immediately obvious that these were the implements used to kill Rabbi Klein. I could make out lengths of thin nylon rope and a small block and tackle, the kind used on yachts to pull up sails. This probably was used to haul his body up into the hanging position.

There was also a big plastic fastener, the kind used to hold cables and things. They were known as 'snap lock' or 'zip ties', except that this one was about a quarter of an inch thick and almost a yard and half long. It could probably hold two substantial logs together. The small loop that had been the noose was cut but I was sure it had only been severed after it had served its grisly purpose. The free end went through a six inch length of rigid plastic tubing and the very end was doubled over and tied to itself to make a handhold. The device was ingenious. The noose created by the fastener could be slipped over the victims head, the rigid tube would be held in your left hand, and your right hand, gripping the handhold, could pull the noose closed. You did not need to be Arnold Schwarzenegger to use the device. As you pulled the fastener, it would ratchet down and choke the victim. Once the noose was in position the perpetrator did not have to use any more strength because the fastener held itself in place.

Diabolical.

Under this stuff were one, maybe two, plastic sheets.

Now I knew why we did not find a urine puddle in the house.

Once the police analyzed these things it wouldn't be long until we knew who the killer was.

I pulled out my phone to call Slatterly and let him know what I had found, when I heard a woman's voice say, "I'll take that."

I turned rapidly expecting to be face to face with Mrs. Alice Weinstein. Instead I saw *Rebbitzen* Klein standing about two yards away holding a small caliber pistol in a very professional two-handed grip. The weapon was aimed towards my central body mass.

Not good.

Why did I allow people to convince me that my gut feelings were wrong?

Never again.

Now I was staring at the wrong end of a firearm.

Very unpleasant sensation.

I had been shot once and looking down the muzzle of a gun brought back a feeling that was much more than déjà vu. It was more like 'danger you'.

"*Rebbitzen* Klein, how nice to see you again," I said with my broadest smile.

"I am sure it is really not so nice for you, but that cannot be helped," she said sternly. "Please give me your phone. Put it on the table and take a step back."

From the size of the bore of the pistol in her hand it looked to be a 22 caliber. The slug did not have a lot of stopping power, but at the range she was from me it would not make much of a difference. Many beginners start off with the 22 because it has less of a kickback and afforded better accuracy. I was surprised that she knew enough to ask me to step away from my phone. Where had she learned to do that? I had been planning on somehow being able to grab her gun. I had no choice but to comply. She picked up my phone and slid it into the pocket of her jacket.

"So it was you, after all," I said.

"Considering I am standing here holding a gun on you in a building that contains the murder weapons, I would say that is a reasonable assumption," said Devorah with a smile. "You are actually quite good at what you do. How did I make that mistake with the length of the rope. Very amateurish on my part and very professional on yours. Congratulations."

Terrific, she is giving me compliments. "It was nothing," I said modestly.

"No it was something. Something that convinced the police that Avraham was murdered," she said nodding her head. "And that is the reason that I have to kill you. I really liked you."

"Yeah like you really liked me when you tried to blow me up or when you sent the Dearborn Jihadists after me."

"I was not trying to kill you," said *Rebbitzen* Klein matter-of-factly. "I was trying to kill Dafna."

"Why did you want to kill her? She was your friend," I said in disgust.

"Because she was the only one that could find what I erased from the computer. That was to be destroyed completely never to be seen again," she said with finality. "She had to die."

"It is commendable that you wanted to prevent people from knowing that your husband was seeking psychiatric help, but we already had the folder from the den so we knew about the inquiries at the private psychiatric clinics."

"I was with my husband when we went to the clinics so I knew what the managers of the different clinics would possibly say. Dr. Felix's files are different."

Why were those files different? Then I remembered that Dr. Felix was still refusing to release the files even though the rabbi was dead. Suddenly it clicked together, "Because the patient was you," I exclaimed. "The rabbi just came along."

"Avraham was always understanding and considerate. He was a good husband in that way," said Devorah apparently letting her thoughts go back to the good days before she ruthlessly killed him. "But then he started saying that either I agreed to be hospitalized or he would divorce me. Neither option could I agree to. I am an excellent *rebbitzen*. I am a perfect *rebbitzen*. Ask anyone. I could not be a psychiatric patient or a divorced *rebbitzen*. That is not me. I could not live like that. He left me no option. Avraham had to die. But I also could not be a murderess. A widowed *rebbitzen* was much more acceptable. At first I had considered using the Dearborn hotheads to kill him but in the end I decided against it because there was the possibility that someone would make my husband into a martyr and I could not have people looking too closely at his death. So I decided that it would be suicide."

She killed him because it would not be proper for her to be a divorcee. Her whole life was just a façade, and she needed it to be perfect. If she could not be the honored wife of a devoted rabbi then the next best thing was to be an honored widow of a devoted rabbi.

She's nuts. Totally nuts.

But obviously cunning.

"How did you get in and out of the house without setting off the alarm?" I wanted to know.

"Bypass switch," she said simply.

"The security company says they never put one in," I countered.

"One of the *Bocherim* is an electronic genius and he did it about five years ago," she said sharing this revelation. "It's hidden behind the cupboards we put up last year. You have to slide your fingers up behind the cupboard."

"Very clever," I said appreciatively. "How did you get out on the night after your husband's funeral? *Rebbitzen* Lipsky was with you."

"She was so thoughtful. What a lovely *neshama* — soul. The *rebbitzen* liked her cup of cocoa before she went to sleep," she said. "Two sleeping pills in the cocoa and she was out cold for the next four hours."

"Once again very clever," I admitted.

"I thought so," she said proudly.

"But I found where you parked this car on the night you killed your husband. The TV station near the theater," I said knowingly.

"Now you are the clever one," said the *rebbitzen*. "But I am afraid, as much as I enjoy this conversation with you,

I must cut it short. As I said before, I did not really want to kill you but I have no other options. You were getting too close."

If Dafna sent me the message over an hour ago the police would probably get here any moment. I had to stall her. "The police know I am here," I said as a warning.

"Do they really?" asked the *rebbitzen*. "If you mean the text message that you received … that was not from the police … that was from me. I used Dafnaleh's telephone."

That sliced through my gut like a sharp knife. If she had used Dafna's phone she could have harmed her. The idea that something bad had happened to her tore me apart. I had to know, "What have you done to Dafna?"

"Nothing yet, but the day is young. You are the first on my agenda," she said.

"Even if you kill me they will find me here and track you down."

"I suppose, eventually they will find you, but I do not expect it will be soon," said the *Rebbitzen* proudly. "I'm going to throw your phone out the window a couple of miles from here. So if they track you through your GPS it won't be to anywhere near here. Your car cannot be seen from the road and if and when they do find you they will assume that you met your death at the hands of my husband's murderer. There is nothing in this building that can be connected to me. Once I get rid of Dafna there is nothing to keep me from continuing on as the honored widow of the great Rabbi Klein." She paused for a moment and looked off in the distance, "You know, I think I will establish a memorial fund in his name and at the annual dinner great rabbis will extol his memory."

Totally, totally nuts.

"If you shoot me someone will hear the shots and report it," I said lamely, trying to figure how I could get close enough to get at the gun.

"I doubt it. I have been doing target practice out here for months and no one has shown the least bit of interest."

"You will never get away with this," I warned her.

"Oh, but I think I will," she said with a grin. "It's been nice to know you, but as Eli Wallach said in the 'Good, the bad, and the ugly' ... when you have to shoot, shoot don't talk."

The first bullet hit me in the left side of the chest. It literally was like a sledgehammer hitting my ribs. I knew that central mass gunshot wounds did not kill straight off. You had a few minutes until you bled out. I had no idea what had been injured but remembering back to the anatomy charts from our first aid courses I knew that my lungs, spleen, and heart were all in that area. Reflexively, I doubled over and reached up to grab at my chest when the second bullet hit me. She must have jerked her hand because this slug hit me in the head. I felt the sting on the right side of my forehead and I saw my hat fly away. Two thoughts ran through my brain for a fraction of a second. The first was, 'My $200 hat is ruined' and the second was, 'I'm totally screwed'.

My world went black.

CHAPTER TWENTY FOUR — *Hydrogen*

I WAS COMING OUT of it. I do not know out of what, but I was coming out.

I had not seen my life pass before my eyes.

I just had not been here.

But now I was coming back.

I had yet to accomplish the feat of opening my eyes and I did not know what I would see when I did. It could be I would open my eyes and thank God for my last two and a half years of learning Torah and doing *mitzvos* — good deeds — and that because of them my life had been spared and I would once again take part in the joys of the world. Or I would open my eyes to see God and the ministering angels welcoming me into *Olam HaBah* — the world to come.

I remembered getting shot and I still felt the pain in my chest and head.

My eyes fluttered open.

God and the ministering angels would have to wait.

All I saw was the inside of the old barn and the white Chevy in its center. I was lying supine on some dirty sacking material so that my head and chest were raised slightly. I suppose I was lying in the very spot I fell after I was shot. Everything looked red tinged and I realized that my eyes were covered in the blood that was running down from my head wound. I brought up my right hand to wipe away some of the blood in my eyes and this caused great pain in my left chest area.

Rebbitzen Klein was gone.

When I sat up I found that blood was still dripping from my nose and chin.

There was blood everywhere.

I must look a fright.

I pushed my right hand inside my blood drenched jacket to feel the damage caused by the gunshot wound to my left chest. The area was remarkably tender and I was sure a couple of ribs were broken. I was extremely surprised not to feel any breaks in the skin and that there was no blood.

What the heck?

I looked at my jacket and saw the bullet had entered on the left side, but when I checked the internal lining I saw the bullet had not penetrated all the way through. Since I knew that my *bocher*'s uniform was not made of Superman material I sought a different explanation. Confused, I reached into my inside jacket pocket and extracted my small *siddur*. There was a 22 caliber slug stuck in its pages. It had almost gotten through the book, but not quite.

Baruch HaShem — praise be to God ... and dinky 22 caliber bullets.

Rabbi Kalmonowitz had once told me that if I said my prayers every day it would unquestionably change my life.

He was not wrong.

More money in the bank.

I climbed shakily to my feet, and I realized I was weak from loss of blood. I had to stop the bleeding from my head.

Everything in the place was filthy.

How unlike *Rebbitzen* Klein not to have cleaned every square inch.

But I suppose she left everything like this just to confuse the police.

I took off my jacket and tore out strips of the lining which was still clean. I wadded up some of the material and pressed it against my head. I assumed that my head wound was just a long graze of the scalp, because the other option was that there was a bullet lodged somewhere in my skull.

I had nothing to lose.

If there was a slug playing hide and seek inside my calabaza I had only a little time left before I said hello to the ministering angels.

Might as well make the best of it while I can.

I secured the makeshift bandage tightly around my head using my tie and this seemed to staunch most of the bleeding. The remaining material was used to clean up my face as best I could.

I noticed that there were a few items that seemed out of place because they were the only things in the building not covered in a layer of dirt and dust. These included a gallon jug of muriatic acid, about a three pound bag of zinc powder, and a bag of large colored party balloons. All three were about half empty. There were also some large empty glass jars and rubber tubing.

What did the *rebbitzen* do with this stuff?

I staggered down to the little stream and drank some water. I had no idea if the stream was polluted but I was consumed with thirst. I splashed water on my face and hands and tried to wash off some of the blood. My shirt had streaks of red all over but there was nothing I could do about it. *Rebbitzen* Klein must have thought she had killed me because the keys to the Hyundai were still in my pants pocket. My optimism was short lived because when I got to the car I found the two front tires were slashed.

Somehow I got to the road.

I knew that I did not have the strength to make it into town on foot so I just stood under the shade of one of the trees waiting for someone to come along.

I have no idea if I waited for thirty seconds or thirty minutes but eventually a new Toyota pickup stopped and the driver asked, "Hey buddy do you need any help?"

I almost laughed out loud. I must look a sight, with my crazy head bandage and blood all over, and he asked if I need any help. I wanted to say, 'No thanks, I'll be fine. I'm just waiting to go to a Halloween party'. Instead I opened the door and said, "Yeah, I do. I've been shot."

I had trouble climbing up into his high cab but once I was in I felt a moment of relief. I was making a mess of his new truck but I could not care less. I knew I was weak from loss of fluids and blood and turned to the driver, "Have you got any water?"

"I think it is not a good idea to drink if you have been shot," said the driver.

"If I don't get something to drink I am going to pass out," I said matter-of-factly.

"In that case, here you go," said the fellow handing me a half gallon bottle of mineral water. "I'm taking you to the hospital."

I finished the first half of the bottle and said, "Good idea." Then I polished off the second half.

We were driving towards the medical center and I felt the water giving me a little strength. Suddenly I remembered the *rebbitzen*'s threat. Dafna was next on the agenda. I asked the driver, "Can I borrow your phone."

"Sure," said the driver and gave it to me.

I called Dafna's cell but once again it went directly to her voicemail. I could not remember her home phone number because that number had been in my phone and my phone was now in some field in Shiawassee County. In today's digital world no one remembers more than a half dozen phone numbers because they are all programmed into their phones. One of the numbers I did remember was Chuckie Short, my computer man from the Detroit PD.

I dialed his number and got his usual, "Yo! Speak to me."

"Chuckie, this is Sy Lincoln," I started.

Chuckie broke in with, "What the hell are you doing out there in East Lansing? World War III? I can't believe what I'm hearing."

"Chuck, I'll fill you in when I can but now this is an emergency. A real emergency, no fooling around," I said sternly.

"I'm here."

"I have to get in contact with Dafna Lachler right now and her cell is not working. Have you got her home phone number?" I asked.

"I always call her cell, but I will get that number for you ASAP."

"Also could you have Sheldon, from CSI give me a call right now," I requested.

"Will do on both of those. I have your number on the display. Give me a minute," he said.

Sheldon was just about the biggest science nerd I had ever met. He was well-versed in just about every branch of medicine and the exact sciences. If anyone knew what you got when you mixed zinc powder and muriatic acid it would be Sheldon.

The phone rang after about sixty seconds and it was Sheldon on the line, "Sy ... you need some help?"

"I haven't got time to explain, but what do you get when you mix zinc powder with muriatic acid?" I asked.

"You get an exothermic reaction. Meaning it gives off a lot of gaseous vapor and heat."

"Is the vapor poisonous?" I wanted to know.

"As far as it being poisonous, muriatic acid is another name for hydrochloric acid and you would not want to get it on your skin. It is very corrosive and will cause burns," he explained.

This was not getting me anywhere. "What about if I threw in some latex party balloons. Does that ring a bell?"

"It sure does," he said excitedly. "It's a well known demonstration of the properties of hydrogen gas. When you mix muriatic acid with zinc powder it produces hydrogen gas. You do this in a closed system and feed the gas through a rubber tube to fill up the balloon. You tie off the balloon and the balloon floats just like helium."

"Is it dangerous?" I asked.

"Damned right it is. It's highly explosive and combustible," he warned. "Did you ever hear about the Hindenburg Zeppelin that exploded in New Jersey in the thirties? That was hydrogen gas. That's why science teachers only use one balloon."

"Science teachers know how to make this stuff?" I asked.

"Sure," said Sheldon. "Great theater. They attach a lighted candle to a stick and put it close to the balloon and ... blam. Impresses the hell out of the kids."

Devorah Klein had been a science teacher.

"What if I used ten balloons?" I inquired.

"Same thing only ... bigger blam. But you would also have a big fire and a big hole in something," he said.

That is what the *rebbitzen* had planned.

Was I too late?

"Thanks, Sheldon. You have been a big help," I said.

"Chuck gave me that number you wanted," said Sheldon.

He gave me Dafna's home phone number and after he hung up I dialed the number with great trepidation. With each ring my heart sank lower and lower. Dafna picked up on the sixth ring, "Hello."

What a relief, "Dafna, this is Sy, ..."

"Sy where have you been?" she interrupted. "I've been calling for more than an hour. I want ..."

I interrupted her in return, "Stop talking and listen." When she complied, I asked, "Has *Rebbitzen* Klein been to your house since I left this morning?"

Dafna did not answer my question instead she said, "Sy, she did it. You were right. She killed Rabbi Klein. I found the material in the doctor's files."

"I know. I tried to call you but it did not go through."

"She used my phone when she was here and since then it does not work,"

"She was there?" I asked nervously.

"A couple of hours ago."

"Did she bring over any balloons?" I asked anxiously.

"How do you know about the balloons?"

"Well, did she?" I had to know.

"Yeah, she came over here all happy and smiley and told me they were for a surprise birthday party for a child in the hospital. What a faker."

"How many balloons," I demanded.

"About two dozen colorful helium balloons tied to a little weighted box. She said she would come to get them later."

The box had to be the detonator.

"Where did you put them?"

"I didn't put them anywhere, she did. They are down in the basement," said Dafna.

"Anywhere near the propane tank?" I asked.

"Right next to it," was her reply.

What should I tell her? There was going to be a big explosion. If I told them to get out of the house, would they get far enough away to be safe? I made a quick decision.

"Don't ask any questions just do as I say," I commanded. "You are in danger. The balloons are explosive. Do not touch them. Take your mother and the girls into the Vault and close the door tightly behind you. Don't come out unless you hear from me or one of the public safety people."

She started to say, "But ..."

"No buts, just do it," I said beseechingly.

I turned to the driver who had been listening to my calls, "I'll give you a hundred bucks if you take me to Charles Street just off Elizabeth."

"What about the hospital?" he asked.

"This is more important. If I made it this far, I'll last a few more minutes."

He made a slight course correction and we were on our way to Dafna's house.

I called 911 and told them there was a strong possibility that there would be an explosion at Dafna's house. The operator did not know how to process the call. I was reporting a situation that had not yet occurred. She discussed this with me and her superior for about three minutes.

Three minutes of valuable time

The discussion became mute when we, and just about half of the Lansing area, heard the loud explosion that rocked the city.

I hoped I had made the right decision and was not too late.

CHAPTER TWENTY FIVE — All Gone

IT TOOK A WHILE to get through the traffic snarls near Dafna's house and when he got about a block away we found the area cordoned off. Police, Fire & Rescue, and medical teams were spread out on the street and adjacent lawns. The firemen were dousing water on the burning remains of Dafna's house. Surprisingly, after the initial one hundred foot fireball, the flames had died rapidly.

Most likely due to the dispersal of the propane gas.

Looks like the tank had almost been empty after all.

Most of Dafna's house was just not there.

All in all it could have been much worse. People with cuts from the flying glass were being treated by the busy medics. The surrounding trees had singed foliage but they all looked like they would live. The homes facing the blast had their windows punched in. None of the surrounding buildings had caught fire but a few would need paint jobs.

Fire & Rescue would not let anyone near the burning building so I could not get information about survivors from Dafna's house. TV and radio crews had set up their broadcast trucks and the reporters were walking about interviewing all the neighbors. Each station was giving exclusive coverage and all the latest information concerning the blast.

As usual ... no one had a clue.

One of the medics saw my blood soaked shirt and the bandage on my head and hustled me over to his ambulance.

I might as well get treated while I waited.

I was consumed with concern.

She could not be hurt. It was unthinkable.

The medic carefully removed my bandage and to make conversation asked me, "Where were you when this happened?"

"About three miles from here," I said honestly, my eyes riveted on the firemen as they worked.

When the bandage came off, the EMT tech seemed to know that he was dealing with a GSW, "How did you get this wound?"

"Gunshot. Probably a 22 but it could have been a 25 caliber. I'm not sure," I answered honestly.

The tech put a clean bandage on my head and made me hold it in place with my hand, "Hold that. I'll be right back."

After maybe five minutes, I can't be sure, because all my attention was on Dafna's house, I heard Slatterly's gruff voice, "I should have known it was you. You're just like a bad penny. At least you weren't in the house."

"Good to see you too," I said sarcastically. It was the best I could do to try and lighten the dark depressed mood I was in.

"Who shot you?" he asked.

"I'll tell you when I know what happened in that explosion," I told him as I stared straight ahead.

"If your gunshot has anything to do with the Klein murder, you have got to tell me. You're withholding evidence," he warned.

"Believe me, whether you know, or don't know who shot me, it is not going to make a big difference in this case," I said confidently.

"You also gotta go to the hospital. A gunshot wound to the head is no joke," he emphasized.

"Do I look like I'm laughing. I'll go to the medical center once I know what happened to the Lachler family," I said grimly.

"You mean, once you know what happened to Mrs. Lachler," he said knowingly.

I thought about what he had just said and then nodded, "Yeah, I guess so."

∞

I had no idea if the Vault had enough air to sustain four people for over an hour. Nor did I know if the concrete walls could withstand the force of the initial blast. So many unknowns.

I could only hope.

Finally the firemen declared the fire out and would allow the rescue teams to approach.   Slatterly somehow commandeered a Fire & Rescue overcoat and helmet for me and I was able to get near the remains of the building. The captain of the crew was telling his men that it was unlikely there were any survivors but instructed them to go through the wreckage to retrieve bodies if there were any.

You have got to be wrong.

I had an advantage that they did not have. I knew where the Vault was located in all this wreckage. The blast had thrown up most of what had been just above the propane tank. So, that meant that the area in front of the door was relatively clear. There was still debris covering the Vault door so no one had seen it yet, but I knew it was there. The problem was how to get down into the basement since the stairs had been blown to kingdom come. I saw a fireman with a ladder and I grabbed it from his arms. Before he could protest too loudly I got it set firmly on the basement floor and was scampering down. Grabbing at debris and burnt wood I tried to clear the way to the door but my ribs were hurting like the dickens and I was not very effective. "Someone help me," I shouted.

People saw what I was doing and within moments half a dozen firemen were at my side moving the smoldering remains that were in front of the door. Another dozen were standing above us on the basement wall offering suggestions as we worked. Once the door was cleared enough for it to open, I rapped loudly on the door but I was not sure that anyone could hear us.

The door opened a crack and then we helped to swing it open further.

Dafna stood at the door, with her mother and two daughters.

I had never been so happy to see anyone in my life.

The Lachler family, none the worse for wear, stood mesmerized as they looked at the soot covered apparitions standing outside the Vault door. Then Dafna stepped forward and stared wide-eyed at the destruction and debris, "What happened to my house?"

"It's just undergoing a little remodeling," I said facetiously.

"A little remodeling, my *tuchis*! It's not here," she said. Then she understood the gravity of the situation and she became frightened, "Oh my God."

Then she began to cry.

"It's okay, you're safe now. We've got you," I said emotionally.

Maybe I was crying as well.

A few things happened at the same time.

Cheers broke out from the firemen and security people, the news broadcasters told the world of the miraculous rescue of the Lachler family, and I took Dafna in my embrace.

I of course knew that a *yeshiva bocher* was not supposed to do things like that but Dafna also knew about that rule and she did not seem to mind. Whatever the reason, even with my aching ribs getting crushed, it felt good. She held me and I held her. There was a transfer of unspoken emotion that was indescribable. I am sure that some of the cameramen got video of me hugging her for the second time in 24 hours and very likely we would become national celebrities. But considering that most of the people in the *yeshiva* world did not watch TV ... who cared.

Tuchis-kicking partners should be allowed to hug.

We were helped up the ladder and out of the basement. The medics checked out the Lachler family for smoke inhalation or any possible injury and they were found to be perfectly healthy. Once it was determined that there had been no one else in the house, the Fire & Rescue teams began folding up all their equipment. The police were running crime scene tape around the property, the TV crews were departing, and the number of gawkers was diminishing rapidly.

Slatterly came over and asked, "You ready now?"

"Yeah. It's time," I said returning my coat and helmet to the firemen.

Dafna saw my bandage, "What happened to you?"

"That's what I want to know," said the cop.

I looked at them both and said accusingly, "*Rebbitzen* Devorah Klein."

Dafna became very angry, "I'll kill that bitch." Then realizing what she had just said, "Please excuse me for using that word."

Slatterly seemed amused and I said, "You are excused and the word fits perfectly."

The cop asked, "So, she's the one who killed the rabbi?"

"Yup," I said with a nod.

"And you have proof?" he asked.

"Murder weapon and everything."

"And she shot you?" asked the cop.

"Twice," I stated.

"She shot you?" asked Dafna incredulously.

"I'm fine," I said belittling my injuries.

"Where else were you hit?" she wanted to know.

I pulled my *siddur* from my pants pocket and showed them the slug lodged in the prayer book.

Slatterly moved away angrily and said, "I'm going to get an arrest warrant and find that ... you'll excuse the expression ... bitch."

"No need," I said. "Do you have your car near here?"

∞

Mrs. Kalin had already taken over the care of her granddaughters and they went with *Rebbitzen* Lipsky to her home.

We rode over to the Klein home in Slatterly's car.

"I haven't got a search warrant," stated the cop. "I don't want her to get off on a technicality. I can't go in there."

"I'm almost certain you won't need it," I told Slatterly. "But to be safe, you stay outside for five minutes after we get in. If I don't come out to warn you off, you can come in."

"Will I need backup," he asked.

"I doubt it," was my answer.

Dafna and I went up to the front door and rang the bell. We waited for about two minutes but no one came to the door. "How will we get in," asked Dafna.

"Most probably the door is not locked," I said pointing to the door.

Dafna turned the handle and the door opened. "How did you know?"

"I know Devorah Klein. I know what she would do," I said sadly.

"Where is she?" asked Dafna.

"Follow me," was all I said and I headed for the steps down to the basement.

As I expected the late *Rebbitzen* Devorah Klein was swaying back and forth ever so gently, suspended from the rope that was tied around her neck.

Dafna retreated a step, brought her hands up to her mouth and said, "Oh my God."

There was a piece of rope tied around her dress just below her knees. She had to be modest until the last. There was a plastic sheet spread on the floor beneath her body with a small puddle of urine in its center. I pointed at the sheet, "That's where our 'puddle of pee' went. When she killed her husband, she put a plastic sheet under the body."

"Where did she kill him?"

"In his bed I suspect. She slid him along the floor with another plastic sheet. It slides pretty well over carpeting.

Getting down the stairs was the tough part and that is the reason for the injury to his heels. She hauled him up with a little block and tackle and then put on the noose."

"But how did she have the strength to choke him. She is a little woman," declared Dafna.

"She designed an ingenious contraption for that. I'll show it to you, some day."

"If she killed him in his bed there must have been some sign of his struggle," she argued.

"There probably was," I agreed.

"So, why didn't the police see it?" she wanted to know.

"Because *Rebbitzen* Klein, remade the bed and covered any signs that might have been there," I explained. "Next day she simply changed the bedding and it was all washed away. Would you look for signs of a struggle in a perfectly made bed."

"No," she admitted.

"Neither did the police."

"But why did she kill herself now," asked Dafna.

"The TV stations have been broadcasting non-stop from your house. She probably followed what was happening on her computer. When she saw that she had not been successful in killing you, she had no other option," I answered.

I heard Slatterly come down the steps. He took one look at the body and said, "Holy crap."

"You don't need backup, you need the coroner," I told the cop.

Slatterly called his staff and they called the county coroner. When he was finished he said, "There is a note over here."

We stepped over to a small table and there was a single sheet of paper covered with the *rebbitzen*'s perfect penmanship. The note said, 'I thought I could go on without my husband, but I was mistaken. May *HaShem* forgive me for what I have done.'

Dafna nodded her head as if realizing something for the first time, "Did you notice that she never lied ... every time we spoke with her ... she never lied ... she just bent the truth. Even in her last message in this world, she did not lie."

"She was insane," I said. "As long as she did not utter an untruth, she thought that it was perfectly all right. She could bend the truth and omit the truth and she was convinced that she was not lying. She did the most despicable things but in her mind she thought that what she did was absolutely reasonable."

"That's what it said in Dr. Felix's files," she said.

"Who is Dr. Felix?" asked Slatterly.

"We'll show you that later," I said to the cop. Then I turned to Dafna, "Why were they going to the shrink?"

"The doctor's notes say that Devorah had been mentally ill since childhood. She had even been hospitalized in her youth. She hid the fact that she was on medication and everything else from Avraham Klein before the marriage. After they were married she tried to use her OCD to be the most perfect of *rebbitzens*."

"That's exactly what she said to me," I said in agreement.

"Do you know why they never had kids?" Dafna asked. When I shook my head she continued, "Because they never had relations. Nothing."

"What kind of a man was the rabbi? Why didn't he divorce her? I mean, twenty years! Holy cow," said the cop.

"Because Rabbi Klein realized that she would not be able to live being a divorced *rebbitzen*. It would not go over well in the community. It was not suitable for her. So he went with her for treatments in the hope of making her better. He did not want to shame her by making any of her problems public."

"But ... twenty years? That's unbelievable," said Slatterly.

"Rabbi Klein was a special person," said Dafna sadly.

I continued with, "I suspect everything came to a head after her little escapade at the Hillel House. She told me he wanted her to be hospitalized or he was going to divorce her. Both options were unacceptable to her. Better to be the widow of a rabbi that committed suicide."

"Is she also the one who planted the grenade and got those Arabs to come kill you?" asked Slatterly.

"That was her," I said. "But I was not the target. She wanted to kill Dafna."

"Me?" exclaimed Dafna. "Why me?"

"Because she did not want anyone to see Dr. Felix's files. You were a threat to her," I explained.

Slatterly said, "Once the others get here I am going to take you to the medical center."

"What are you going to do about this?" Dafna asked both of us.

"About what?" asked the cop.

"We three know that Devorah Klein killed her husband," she said. "But we also know that she was totally crazy. I'm no lawyer, but it sounds to me that if she ever stood trial she would probably be found not guilty by reason of insanity."

"Possibly," said Slatterly.

"Probably," I said.

"Now, I know that you both want to uphold truth, justice, and the American way. You want to make criminals pay for their crimes," she said taking a pause. "But ... and I ask you to hear me out ... what good will it do to tell the world that Devorah Klein was a murderess? Why can't we just let everyone think she took her own life because she was depressed by her husband's death?"

"Because, she was not depressed. She carefully planned the whole thing and that makes it premeditated murder. She has to pay," said the cop.

"But, why?" I asked, realizing what Dafna was saying. "She is not going to pay. She's dead. There is no insurance money or inheritance that is going to be scammed or anything. Letting the world know that this happened won't prevent another person from committing a similar crime. She was crazy. I even have a feeling that your police chief won't allocate the funds or manpower to conduct a full investigation because what does society gain by making all this public? Rabbi Klein lost his life because he did not want to embarrass his wife. If we make all this public ... in a sense ... we will be demeaning the great sacrifice he made."

"It's the law," said Slatterly defensively.

"And the law is a crock sometimes," I said. "Haven't you ever worked on a case ... caught the slime ball that did the crime ... and then seen him walk because of a loop hole in the law?"

We could hear the police crews entering the house.

"I'll have to think about it," said the cop. "Temporarily, I'm calling this a suicide. Now let's get you to the hospital."

∞

Slatterly offered to take Dafna to the Lipsky house but she insisted she wanted to stay with me. I was x-rayed, had a CT scan, was poked and prodded and the doctors said that I had a hairline fracture in my skull.

Good thing I have always been thick-headed.

There were two broken ribs on the left side of my chest and the beginning of a huge black and blue mark that went right down to my belly button. One of the ER docs stitched the gap on the right side of my scalp and told me I would have an interesting scar when I started to go bald.

Since my blood pressure and pulse were almost normal they decided that I did not need to get a blood transfusion to get my blood count back to normal. Good food, rest and relaxation would do just as well. In the end I was connected to an IV and kept for the night because I had been knocked out by the head injury and the dictums of the hospital's insurance policy said that I was not allowed to be discharged directly.

When I insisted that I was fine and that Dafna should go home to be with her daughters, she said, "I haven't got a home anymore. Might as well spend the night here."

The effects of the concussion were such that I dozed most of the time, but whenever I opened my eyes it was comforting to see Dafna sitting there.

∞

Morning arrived in East Lansing and without my *tallis* and *tefillin* I would have to say my prayers without them. At 7:30 am, Slatterly showed up and solved the problem because the state police had returned the items from my blown up car the evening before. The picnic hamper was in pieces but the *tallis* and *tefillin* were fine. The doctors discharged me and a nurse's aide put me in a wheelchair and conveyed me to the entrance.

Another hospital dictum.

Throughout it all Dafna had been at my side.

Well, maybe not all the time, because her car, with a few scorch marks on the paint, was sitting in the parking structure. She must have gone to get it.

So, okay, she had been there most of the time.

I found that I liked that very much.

I was helped into her car and as we drove away from the hospital, I asked, "What are you going to do now?"

"I'm going to take you to your hotel for now," she said.

"After you drop me off."

"You mean without a roof over our heads?" she asked.

Typical Jewish answer. Ask another question.

"Yeah, your house is gone."

"Well, because of the Vault, my business is still intact. So that won't be a problem," she stated. "I'll be able to be back in business without too much of a problem. I realized this morning that today is Friday and that we have no place to be for *Shabbos*, but then *Rebbitzen* Kalmonowitz called and invited us to spend *Shabbos* with them. So, we are going to go to Detroit as soon as I drop you off. We'll move into our house in Detroit for now. After all, it is just sitting there empty. Hopefully we'll get settled in by two o'clock and that should give us enough time to rush to the mall to get clothes before sunset and the start of *Shabbos*. All our belongings and stuff were either burned or blown up."

I just realized that it was indeed Friday morning, and since I had not been in the *bais medrash*, I had not received a *Shabbos* invitation from any of the rabbis or the married *bocherim*. I had to get back to the city and scrounge some food for *Shabbos*. No more meals from Mrs. Kalin.

No more Dafna.

That will be strange.

I really liked seeing her and having her near me. The excitement of these past few days should last her a lifetime so that she could now retire from her illustrious career as a detective and get back to her business and family. Looks like I'll just have to file this whole week to the pleasant memories file at the back of my brain. She has to get her life back on track.

Interestingly, she will be in Detroit this weekend, "So you'll be spending some time in Detroit," I stated.

"I really should have moved back when David died. I was just procrastinating. Aliza and Susie really should also be in the girls school in Detroit."

I understood her immediately, "You did not want to give up his memory. Too many good things associated with the house."

"Nothing so noble," she admitted. "I was just hiding out here. Before he died, David, made me promise that I would leave East Lansing and start a new life. I was just scared."

"Do you think you are ready now?" I asked tentatively.

She kept her gaze out the windshield as she drove and said, "Yes, things have changed. I'm ready now."

"How have they changed?" I probed.

"Definitely for the better," she said.

"So, are there good things in your life now," I questioned.

"Really good things," she said with a sly smile keeping her eyes fixed straight ahead.

"Where is your house in Detroit?"

"About four blocks from your condo," she said blandly.

Whammy.

Of course, she knew where I lived.

She hacked my personnel files.

The idea that she would be living near me, made me feel good. It put a new perspective on my future.

"That's really good, because you promised to cook me a dinner, so that will be really convenient."

She still did not look in my direction but said with a smile, "Yeah, really convenient."

EPILOGUE

I CHECKED OUT OF the motel and took my bags down to the Hyundai. It had been towed and was now equipped with two new tires. As I put my bags in the back seat, I reflected over the Rabbi Klein case. Slatterly had consulted with his boss and it was decided that Rabbi Klein's death would be classified as a homicide with assailant unknown and officially the case was closed. *Rebbitzen* Klein was classified as a suicide, which it was, and there would be no further investigation into her connection with the death of her husband. No one had decided what to do with her booby-trapping my car or her instigating the Jihadist attack or blowing up Dafna's home, but for now there would not be an active investigation.

It was now almost noon and I knew that *Rebbitzen* Klein's funeral had taken place in Detroit earlier this morning.

She would be buried next to her 'beloved' husband.

So the whole affair was now officially behind us.

Since we parted this morning Dafna had called me two times. The first time to tell me that she finally located Alice Weinstein. We were unable to find her because she had been hospitalized for quite a while in a mental institution. The second time to tell me about how to return her husband's *tefillin* and about the *rebbitzen*'s burial arrangements. Just passing on information she said, but we both knew different. Now she was on her way to Detroit. The good thing about having your house blown into tiny little pieces was that you did not have to pack much.

I was going around dressed only in a white shirt and *yarmulke* because my *yeshiva bocher* uniform had been ruined by *Rebbitzen* Klein when she made me the target for her shooting escapade. My spare outfits were in Detroit.

The case was over and I took satisfaction in having solved it. I missed that feeling. I would have to see how I could combine detective work with learning in the *bais medrash*.

Just as I hit the ignition and the small motor chugged into life, my cell phone rang.

I was surprised to hear Rav Kalmonowitz's voice. "*Reb* Shimon, how are you feeling?"

"Fine *Rebbi*. Thank you for asking."

"No, I must be the one to thank you," he said. "I asked you to prove that *Reb* Avraham did not take his own life and you did that superbly. *HaKodesh Baruch Hoo* — literally the most Blessed and Holy-one — God — has given you a talent, you should think about using it more often for the good of others."

Was he reading my mind.

"I'll think about it," I said.

"Are you coming back to Detroit today?"

"Yes, as a matter of fact I am," I said.

"Very good, then you will be our guest for meals this *Shabbos*," said *Rebbi* in a tone which meant I had no choice in the matter.

My food difficulties were solved, "Thank you *Rebbi*."

"I would like to see you," he said.

Uh oh. All my problems started the last time Rabbi Kalmonowitz had asked to see me. What has he got planned for me now? "Certainly *Rebbi*."

"I wanted to especially thank you for what you did for the *rebbitzen*," said Rabbi Kalmonowitz.

He must mean Dafna. I enjoyed working with her and hope to be with her a lot more. "It was nothing. She was a big help to me," I said simply.

"I did not mean Dafna Lachler, although I thank you for that as well. I meant what you did for Devorah Klein. Especially after what she did to you. Your actions showed real compassion and a love of your fellow man. *Yasher koach* — may your strength increase."

How did *Rebbi* know about that? That was supposed to be a secret shared only by the police, myself and Dafna. I knew that both Dafna and I had not told anyone and it was highly doubtful if he had gotten that information from the police.

Rebbi is amazing. He knows things. He feels things most people do not.

Suddenly it dawned on me that Rabbi Kalmonowitz had invited me to his house for *Shabbos* and that Dafna and her family would be there as well. Perhaps I should ask his advice concerning myself and Dafna.

His insight could be helpful.

"*Rebbi* , can I ask you a question?"

"Yes, *Reb* Shimon," he answered.

"You know that Dafna Lachler is moving back to Detroit."

"What a tragedy. Her home was destroyed" he said.

"Well, we worked together ... and we found that we could be very helpful ... one to the other." I was uncertain as to how to continue. "Anyway, she will be needing quite a bit of assitance getting set up in Detroit ... and I sort of ... volunteered to help her."

"What is it you wish to ask of me?" queried *Rebbi* .

"I guess I wanted to know if it was okay. ... helping Dafna Lachler. I don't want to break any *yeshiva* rules or get anyone into trouble."

Rav Kalmonowitz laughed and said, "*Reb* Shimon, *Reb* Shimon. You are such a *tzadik*."

Now that was new one.

Me, a *tzadik*?

"*Rebbi* , believe me," I said. "I am no *tzadik*.

"No, believe me . You are a *tzadik* and you don't even know it," said Rav Kalmonowitz with conviction. "Go help Dafnaleh. She needs your assistance right now and by helping her you will be doing a great *mitzvah*."

"So it is okay to help her," I asked once again to be sure.

"Believe me ... it will be good," said *Rebbi* .

What did he mean by that? What will be good?

"Could you repeat that, *Rebbi* ?" I requested.

"It will be good," said Rav Kalmonowitz softly and broke the connection.

If Rabbi Kalmonowitz said it ... you could take it to the bank.

BIOGRAPHY

Born in the royal palace at Hampton Court, England (it was a maternity hospital at the end of WWII), Melvyn Westreich was raised in New York City. He attended Yeshiva University and completed his medical degree and residencies at Wayne State University, in Detroit. After completing his studies he moved to Israel and eventually became the chairman of the Department of Plastic Surgery at the Assaf HaRofeh Medical Center of Tel Aviv University, Sackler School of Medicine, the President of the Israel Association of Plastic Surgery and the Chairman of the Board of Plastic Surgery of Israel. His interests include travel, photography, gardening and he has a *mishigas* about Japanese Gardens. He presently lives on Kibbutz Yavne, in Israel, with his wife Ada. *Murder in the Kollel*, is his first published novel.

Excerpt from **THE KOSHER BUTCHER**
The next Lincoln/Lachler Mystery
- Soon to be published -

Prologue

"Well, it's about time," thought the murderer seeing the approaching vehicle.

It was unlikely that anyone but his victim would be coming down this dark stretch of road so late in the evening. But, you cannot rely on luck. If someone else does drive by they would remember him standing alongside a stopped car and he would have to abort.

The car appeared to be the right model and make so the murderer waved his arms to flag it down.

The car whizzed by him.

"What kind of driver is that idiot Jew?" thought the murderer. *"Nearly hit me."* Finally the car slowed and stopped. He was happy to see the full beard, black hat and dark suit identifying the driver as the rabbi from the *yeshiva* academy.

"He's perfect," thought the murderer to himself as he walked up to the car.

"Sorry about that — I did not expect to see anyone on the road," said the rabbi apologetically as he rolled down his window.

"That's OK," said the murderer. "At least you stopped."

"What's the problem?" asked the clergyman through the window.

"Boy, am I glad to see you," he said. "Car died and my cell phone doesn't work. Could I borrow your phone to call my road service?"

"Sure, just a second," said the rabbi searching in his pocket and handing the phone through the window to the murderer. "There you go."

"You're a life saver," he said with a smile. The murderer took the phone and began punching in some random numbers as he wandered back towards his own car. "Hey, what's this?" he exclaimed pointing towards the rear of his car.

"What's what?" asked the rabbi sticking his head out the window.

"Boy, am I lucky. Would you look at this? I never would have made it home," said the murderer earnestly.

"What did you find?" asked the clergyman getting out of his car to see if he could help.

"Right here. Look at that," said the murderer pointing at the rear of his car.

"I don't see anything wrong," said the rabbi, leaning over to look under the car.

The murderer slipped the garrote quickly around the rabbi's neck and pulled his arms apart tightening the thin wire loop. "Now you see what's wrong," said the murderer hoisting the victim across his hip to gain leverage and began pulling him off the road into the low bushes.

Other than the scuffling of his heels against the ground the rabbi hardly made a sound as he fought the pressure of the wire about his neck that was crushing his wind pipe and extinguishing his life. He thrashed about for almost four minutes and then became still. The murderer kept the garrote tight for another two minutes just like the instructor in the Ranger course at Fort Benning had demonstrated so many years before.

The murderer hoisted the limp body up onto his shoulder and dumped the now dead Jew into his trunk. He found the wallet in an inside pocket and extracted the thirty dollars in cash. *"I thought all these Jew boys carry oodles of green?"* he thought to himself. He took the wallet and cell phone and dumped them on the front seat of the Jew's car. Then he retrieved the fellow's black hat from where it had fallen on the road and tossed it through the window onto the seat next to the phone and wallet.

Sliding into the front seat of his own car the murderer said out loud, "That went pretty well. Two down and two to go."

Made in the USA
Middletown, DE
31 August 2021